Sand

and other stories

ASHOKAMITRAN

Translated from the Tamil by
N. KALYAN RAMAN and GOMATHI NARAYANAN

Orient BlackSwan

SAND AND OTHER STORIES

ORIENT BLACKSWAN PRIVATE LIMITED

Registered Office
3-6-752 Himayatnagar, Hyderabad 500 029 (A.P.), INDIA
e-mail: centraloffice@orientblackswan.com

Other Offices
Bangalore, Bhopal, Bhubaneshwar, Chennai, Ernakulam, Guwahati, Hyderabad, Jaipur, Kolkata, Lucknow, Mumbai, New Delhi, Patna

First published by Orient Longman Pvt. Ltd. 2002
Reprinted 2004
First Orient Blackswan impression 2009
Tamil edition of **Sand** (*Manal*) was first published in 1974; **Malati** (*Malati*) in 1981; **Those Two** (*Iruvar*) in 1993.
Now reprinted by Rajarajan Pathippakam
in *Ashokamitran Kurunovelgal*

ISBN 13: 978 81 250 2268 8
ISBN 10: 81 250 2268 6

Typeset by
Welkin Computer Centre
Chennai

Printed in India at
Yash Printographics
NOIDA

Published by
Orient Blackswan Private Limited
1/24 Asaf Ali Road
New Delhi 110 002
e-mail: delhi@orientblackswan.com

Ashokamitran (born 1931, Secunderabad) is one of the most distinguished of contemporary Tamil writers. He began his literary career with a prize-winning radio play in 1953, and has since written a number of short stories, novellas and novels. His work has been extensively translated into many Indian and European languages. The major English translations include *Taneer* (*Water*) by KATHA, *Padinettavadu Atchakodu* (*The Eighteenth Parallel*) by Orient Longman, The Colours of Evil by Manas, East West Books.

Ashokamitran lives and works in Chennai. His years of rich and diverse contribution to Tamil literature have brought him many honours and awards, including the Sahitya Akademi award (1996). He was also awarded a creative writing fellowship by the University of Iowa as part of its International Writing Program.

N. Kalyan Raman, a senior telecom professional, took up translation in the mid-90s. His translation of Tamil short stories has been included in several collections of Indian language fiction in translation, including *Southern Harvest* and *KATHA Prize Stories*, published by KATHA. He has also translated a collection of Ashokamitran's short stories, *The Colours of Evil*, published by Manas, East West Books. He lives and works in Mumbai.

Gomathi Narayanan has taught in Kerala and New Delhi. Her translations from Tamil literary materials have appeared in *Indian Literature* (Sahitya Akademi) and other periodicals. She has translated Ashokamitran's *Padinettavadu Atchakodu* (*The Eighteenth Parallel*), published by Orient Longman. She has also translated, with Lakshmi Holmstrom, Sundara Ramaswamy's *Waves*, published by Manas, East West Books. She lives in Chennai.

Contents

Foreword

I have to admit that I read Ashokamitran for the first time, only a year ago. This is a poor comment on the sufficiency of my reading. But on closer scrutiny thereby also hangs a tale concerning the nature of the Indian State, wherein the One inevitably must translate into the Many. It also points to the foolhardiness and fragility of the sponsored neo-myths about the Oneness of Indian Literature and Tradition. If a reasonably book-and-literature-friendly person like me cannot access Ashokamitran or Ananthamurthy or Mahasweta Devi in my time and day unless I maintain a vigilant eye on translations, reviews and new arrivals in bookshops, what about the average Indian whose first concern may not be literature? What's all this about Oneness then?

If any works of imagination provide the connecting link between most Indian languages, they are the *Ramayana* and the *Mahabharata*. These two tough texts have survived adaptation both by religion and television. If they have managed to create a semblance of the so-called Oneness, it is only through translations and transcreations. The translations and versions they have undergone state the perfect case for translating literatures in the Indian subcontinent. Even variant phenomena like the rath yatra and the Ram temple have much to thank those translators for, viewed in retrospect. The *Ramayana* and the *Mahabharata* transmigrated into the folklore of the many Indian cultures through the open door of the mother tongues. Re-tellers of the epics such as Ezhuthachan of Malayalam or Kambar of Tamil became the cornerstones of the formation of a pan-Indian Hinduism. It was not Sanskrit that hit the jackpot but the re-tellings in mother tongues. Thus the *Ramayana* and the *Mahabharata* became the Mothers of all Indian Stories. They set up the Vision of the Story in Indian mother tongues.

Which brings me back to my point about the nature of the Indian State and my predicament as a reader. Oneness has long been the much-flogged slave of patriotism and nationalism. The charming irony of the Indian situation is that the Indian State itself is made up of a thousand Onenesses. The Indian Constitution will make no sense to at least ninety per cent of the Indian population unless translated into the many Onenesses of the mother tongues. The Indian State, for its very survival, demands translation.

It was Gandhi, for the do-or-die purpose of winning freedom, who proposed the daring dream of nationhood to the people inhabiting over 600 native and colonial political entities in and outside the British Indian Empire. Another dreamer, who excelled in romantic but evocative English diction, spent his days in prison writing a book to underwrite the Gandhian dream. No one problematised the fact that the *Discovery of India* by Jawaharlal Nehru—from which most of today's most beaten-up Oneness phrases flow—was written in English. This new mythology and hagiography of the proposed Indian State succeeded enormously because it provided a populist translation/re-telling in English of Gandhi's lawyer-like, dry and disturbingly spiritual design of the nation-dream. How useful were translations! How useful was English to win freedom! And also to paste together the bits and pieces of British India as a nation!

It is wonderful that Indian Oneness becomes real only when it is translated into at least twenty mother tongues. Therefore, even though I could not access Ashokamitran for many years of my reading, I am consoled that it was the many-facedness of India that caused it and not the faceless mask of Oneness. It also makes one humble to realise that all the posturing we tend to do about grasping the 'Indian Reality' is just a lot of humbug. The sooner we accept that we are Many and most probably will remain so, the better for our interconnectivity—and I do not mean that tiresome old phrase, Unity in Diversity. When I read Ashokamitran for the first time—it was his novella *Water* translated into English by Lakshmi Holmstrom—my first impulse was to translate it into Malayalam. Though I never did manage to do that, I think that impulse said a lot about connectivity in the Indian situation. Translate! Or be drowned in the dreary, morbid soup of Oneness!

•———•

I was so moved by *Water* that I sat still for a long time going back over the story to see where Ashokamitran had tied the knot that had bound me hand and foot. I had a hunch then. Now having read the three novellas translated here, my fears, as another writer, are confirmed. Ashokamitran is a master of the art of lying low in the narrative—with utter ruthlessness. By ruthlessness, I do not mean the special ability exhibited by many in Indian politics, but the quality Don Juan advised Carlos Castaneda: 'For a sorcerer, ruthlessness is not cruelty. Ruthlessness is the opposite of self-pity or self-importance. Ruthlessness is sobriety.'[1] Ruthlessly, Ashokamitran leads his characters through a maze of life's ordinary, casual and dull

1. Carlos Castaneda, *The Power of Silence: Further Lessons of Don Juan* (New York: Simon and Schuster, 1987), 174.

details, guiding the reader into the lovely belief that, from the closing of a wicket-gate to the hanging of a shirt on the clothes-hanger, every little thing is part of fate's grand plan. He wastes no pity, gives no quarter. Then like the final straw that broke the camel's back, he would add one more detail. And BOOM! The world explodes with a blinding flash. You are no more the reader you started out as. The illumination has consumed you.

We have seen Hemingway do it. But he does it not by lying low but by forcing your attention with American machismo, packing in journalistic staccato and a sense of controlled drama. I can also recall Salinger's ruthless depiction of the tragic, dressed in a veneer of chitchat, shoptalk and cunning comedy. He creates a narrative so highly charged that it literally crackles with tension, because his people are tense the way only Americans can be. Ashokamitran's people are non-dramatic and pedestrian in a devastating way that only the Tamil brahmin middle class can lay claim to. Lying low, delivering detail after detail with the apparent pitilessness of fate, he stalks them till they are no more opaque and are changed into transparent beings that glow with the soft gleam of the spirit.

It startled me as a writer to see that, often, even at vital turning points in the narrative, Ashokamitran employs no motives or circumstantial reasonings to enable his characters to tide over the transition. For example, Sarojini, Malati, Vaala and Dhanam, the four women who confront the inexorable happenings in the three novellas presented here, travel their excruciatingly pliant paths up Golgotha like fish swimming downstream. The story itself becomes fate. Nothing can be explained or anticipated. Like a lynch mob, the terrifying chores of life surround you—even the making of a cup of coffee takes place in a vale of horrors. But when Ashokamitran lifts the veil of Maya, illuminations burst forth from the drab and crowded living rooms and kitchens of joint families like the great stars rising upon the Milky Way on a clear night.

The strangest thing about Ashokamitran's craft is that he works without any apparent craft. Or he submerges the tools so well that the narrative is almost no different from real life. I am reminded of another piece of advice from Don Juan. I thought it connected to Ashokamitran in a special way because of what I heard him say at the recent international literary meet in New Delhi.[2] He mentioned how, many years ago, he had been making a shaky start in writing while tinkering listlessly with many jobs, until his last boss, in exasperation, shouted at him to quit and start writing for a living. And Don Juan tells Castaneda: 'Of course, you're not a writer, so you will have to use sorcery. First, you must visualise your experiences as if you were reliving them, and then you must see the text in your dreaming. For you, writing should not be a literary exercise, but rather an exercise in sorcery.'[3] But Ashokamitran, having become a writer in every drop of his sweat, uses sorcery for some other ends (we shall address that later).

One of Ashokamitran's secrets perhaps is that he has a sorcerer's hold on two things—the Tamil brahmin joint family, and the psyche of the young middle class Tamil brahmin woman. His infiltration into the marvellous and mind-boggling nexus of the brahmin joint family is an awesome thing. There is not the minutest movement of thought, prayer, human being or object in those suffocating and exhilarating conglomerations of bodies, voices, food, tears, sweat, horoscopes, jewellery, saris, sanitary napkins, pujas, love and ritual, that escapes his attention. It is as if he carries within himself the group-mind with all its overwhelming urges, terrors and sorrows. It is a mind system like a beehive—fragile,

2. *'At Home in the World: International Festival of Indian Literature,'* was organised by the ICCR, New Delhi, February 2002.
3. Castaneda, *Power of Silence*, 14.

vulnerable, vibrant, consistent, tenacious, and wedded to slogging, slogging and slogging. It is moth-eaten into porousness by ritual and tradition. Ashokamitran's characters are wanderers on this great, interpenetrating and fascinating web of orthodoxy, running hard to break free but standing still all the more.

I dread to say this, but I feel that R. K. Narayan, master of the Malgudian middle world, almost never confronted the soul's terrifying loneliness that haunts these realms. Over a period of time he perhaps converted Malgudi into an invention and its people into robots. Malgudi's ordinariness had acquired the unreality of a waxworks village. Malgudi does not lead you to illuminations because, by the very nature of his genius, Narayan did not seek out the terror of the soul in its lairs. But Ashokamitran has known the Dark Lord closely in His hideouts in the bathrooms, kitchens, yards and living rooms of the brahmin family. He does not invite you to a katcheri in pity as he recounts the tales of the survivors. He tells their stories without anger or recrimination, without asking you to a grand beheading, but investing suffering with the possibility of dignity.

Ashokamitran must have been a woman, in not one previous birth, but very many. He moves in under the skin and into the secret places of the heart of his young women with the deftness of a shape-changer and the stealth of a mind-stealer. It is an extraordinary performance. And he did it at a time when almost no one, including women, was talking of a place for women under the soft Indian moon—and the indifferent and patriarchal sun. Sarojini, Malati, the doctor's wife, Sujana, Vaala and Dhanam (and I cannot forget Jamuna of *Water*), are all women engulfed in the unforgiving and relentless web of family, tradition and relationships. Their sorrows and deadly fatigues confront us with a simplicity and inner logic that defies rules, and force us to the edge of our jittery beings. Sarojini's mother dies so quietly—almost like a moth trapped in the house—that her death is an event noticeable only by the minor stir of the post-funeral ceremonies. But somewhere in the background, we hear Sarojini's small voice sobbing to Periyamma, 'I feel scared.'

These are not stories by a conscious feminist. Ashokamitran, like all great writers, transcends theories as he seeks the human heart and pursues the cloud of unknowing that is history. His unforgettable women and the world they inhabit, shine and burn not only for womanhood but for the whole condition of man.

As I said earlier, thank God for translators and the wonderful connectivity they provide! May their tribe increase and multiply! Thank heavens for the readers of translations! May they multiply like the stars in the heavens so that publishers shall feel good! As also authors! Kalyan Raman's translation of *Sand* and *Malati*, and Gomathi Narayanan's of *Those Two* are smooth, comfortable and direct. The structured simplicity of the English they use, has a clean and contemporary feel, and matches the directness of Ashokamitran's Tamil prose (whose flavour I have gathered with the help of Tamil friends). Dialogues, normally difficult to handle, are live and fresh. I congratulate the translators and the publisher for bringing these lovely stories into the vast realm of international readership.

17 May 2002

PAUL ZACHARIA
Thiruvananthapuram

Sand

There was nobody on the front veranda when Sarojini opened the gate. Instead of going in directly, she went around the house. She dumped her books through the open window in the hall before she reached the well in the backyard. There was a newly strung clothesline between the pulley frame at the well and the trunk of the gooseberry tree. Many pieces of baby's clothing, large and small, were hung up to dry. She knew at once who the guest was. Sarojini moved away, carefully avoiding any physical contact with the clothes. She called out, 'Amma!' Had her mother been in the kitchen, she would have heard Sarojini, but she was somewhere else. Sarojini called out again, 'Amma!' This time, too, her mother did not respond.

Muniyamma came instead. 'What's the matter? Have you got your periods?' she asked Sarojini.

'Where is Amma?'

'She is in the hall. Your elder sister has come.'

'I know that. Could you ask Amma to come here?'

Muniyamma went into the house. Amma came out a little later. 'What is it, di?' she asked Sarojini.

'I need hot water for a bath.'

'Karmam, karmam,' Amma mumbled to herself. As she turned to enter the bathroom where a large copper boiler sat on a wood stove, she asked Sarojini, 'Was it a cockroach today, or a toad?'

Sarojini had in fact dissected a cockroach that day. For another four or five lab sessions, she would have to continue with the cockroach. She had to turn it over—and after spreading its legs and pushing aside its wings and mandibles—slice the belly open and lift out the intestinal tract gently with pincers before she could begin her task of examining its reproductive organs and salivary glands under a microscope. And then she would have to draw detailed diagrams in her lab record. The cockroach came after the toad. It would in turn be followed by earthworm, snail, butterfly, fish, rat.... She had to cut open all these and more, and draw diagrams of their insides. Only after attaining some proficiency in cutting up these creatures could she expect to take the scalpel to a human corpse.

Muniyamma brought her a small bucket filled with water from the well. There was no one else at the well, nor was there anyone about in the adjacent backyards. But out there in the open, Sarojini could only wet her handkerchief, which was tied around her dissection box. She then entered the bathroom. The stove was now blazing. If the cauldron had been filled to less than half its capacity, she would have hot water soon. Sarojini kept the dissection box in a corner of the alcove and loosened her blouse. Fortunately, Muniyamma had not filled the cauldron to the brim. Before long, her mother was able to prepare a bucketful of lukewarm water. Muniyamma had to pour the water over Sarojini's head—no one else was available. But it was her mother who brought her petticoat and sari from inside the house on the tip of a long staff, and draped them over the door. Sarojini finished her bath, twisted a towel around her wet hair and came out.

In the hall, Vanaja was sleeping off her fatigue from the journey. Her three children were sprawled all around her, of which only two were asleep. The youngest, Suresh, who was barely a year old, was sucking the rubber nipple of a feeding bottle. Sarojini tiptoed past the sleeping Vanaja. Vanaja was sleeping on her back, with her arms and legs splayed wide from her body. Suresh kept making sucking noises constantly.

Sarojini picked up the books she had pushed in earlier through the window. She stacked them neatly on her table which was wedged below the staircase on the veranda. Even so, it was a cosy little nook, affording privacy and quiet. But at night, mosquitoes always buzzed around, ready to gorge themselves.

Sarojini went back to the bathroom and took the dissection box, which she carried in her left hand. Amma was roasting appalams in the kitchen. There were intermittent sounds of snoring from Vanaja. If she slept on her side, the snoring might perhaps even cease. But after her third child, she had gained a lot of weight and began sleeping on her back. She slept with her limbs spread-eagled like a scarecrow. Sarojini wondered if she too would start sleeping like that at some point in her life.

There was a loud noise as though the gate was being smashed to pieces. Her eldest brother, Mani, was back. He came cycling home from his office at five thirty sharp. He went out after having his tiffin and coffee, and was seldom back before ten or even ten thirty. Her other brother, Appu, also owned a bicycle. He played tennis every evening. Even though he spent a fair amount of time chatting with his friends after the game, he grew bored by seven or seven thirty. He would then come home, have his tiffin along with his supper and go to bed.

Vanaja had woken up and greeted Mani. Catching sight of Sarojini, she exclaimed in the same breath, 'When did *you* come?'

'Did you come by the passenger train? We had no idea,' Mani sounded surprised as he leaned his bicycle against the wall. As soon as his back was turned, the bicycle collapsed on the floor. 'Saniyan,' he cursed as he picked it up and placed it against the wall, careful this time.

From the kitchen, Amma called out, 'Di, Saroja, why don't you put this tiffin down your throat and be done with it?'

'Wait a minute, Amma. I'm coming too,' said Mani.

'Oh, you've come,' said Amma.

Mani removed his shoes and flung them towards one corner of the hall. Suresh sat up. 'Why do you keep sticking this rubber thing into his mouth? It looks obscene,' said Mani irritably. Without a word, Vanaja removed the rubber from the child's mouth and wiped it with her sari.

'This is just a casual visit, I suppose?' asked Mani. He was changing into a veshti. Suresh began to bawl, now that he had lost the solace of the rubber nipple. Mani glared at him.

Vanaja told Sarojini, 'Why don't you pick him up and keep him for a while? He won't cry then.' For a child barely a year old, Suresh was fairly big. He tried to struggle free when Sarojini picked him up, kicking at her with both his legs. She held him tight.

As Mani wore his veshti in a haphazard fashion and rushed to the backyard, he stopped for a moment to ask Vanaja again, 'Athimber is doing fine, isn't he? This is just a casual visit, then?'

'I felt like seeing all of you, so I came down. Now I can live here in peace for at least a couple of months,' replied Vanaja.

'Two months? What happens to Athimber? How will he manage?'

'Oh, what's he got to worry about? He has a maid to sweep and mop the floors. He cooks his own food or sends for it from the club. He doesn't have any of my normal problems—

doesn't have to rock the crib, wash the baby's rags or feed the children. No worries at all.'

Mani left quickly after hearing Vanaja's reply. Sarojini went to the kitchen. Amma had served uppuma in two small plates. 'Call Vanaja,' she told Sarojini.

Sarojini went to call Vanaja, carrying Suresh with her. Vanaja was dropping the rubber nipple from Suresh's feeding bottle into a wicker basket. Sarojini told her, 'Amma wants you.'

'I'll be there in a minute,' said Vanaja. She had an urgent question for Sarojini, 'Tell me about the sari you bought for Deepavali.'

Sarojini had no immediate answer.

'You did buy saris for Deepavali, didn't you?' asked Vanaja again.

Sarojini replied this time 'No.'

'Why not?'

'Appa and Amma didn't buy any of us new clothes this year. Only Bhavani got a new sari because it was her first Deepavali after marriage. Athimber got a veshti.'

Bhavani was younger than Vanaja, and two years older than Appu. After a long and nearly hopeless struggle, her marriage had taken place in August last year. There was only a difference of one-and-a-half years between Vanaja and Bhavani, but by the time Bhavani was eventually married, Vanaja had had three children.

'How much did they pay for her sari?'

'A hundred and forty, or fortytwo, I think.'

Vanaja rolled her eyes and pouted.

Amma called out, 'Ei, Vanaja, Saroja, where have you gone?' At this, Vanaja went to the kitchen, Sarojini following her. There, Mani was already well into his uppuma.

Vanaja asked her mother, 'Amma, is there some milk left, apart from what you've used to set the curd?'

'I've saved some. Why do you ask?'

'When the children wake up, give them milk. They will never go to sleep if you give them coffee or tea.'

Sarojini also helped herself to some uppuma. While eating, she remembered the cockroach, but her stomach did not turn. Suresh had left her side, he was now standing in front of Vanaja, whining. Vanaja did not spare him even a tiny morsel. Mani tried to give him some, but Vanaja wouldn't let him. 'No, no, don't. It's not good for his stomach,' she said firmly.

When Sarojini was busy gathering and sweeping the crumbs and discarded rings of green chilli from the floor, Renuka came barging in. She had come to give Sarojini a book she had asked for. When Sarojini's mother asked her if she would have some tiffin, she declined, 'No, mami. My brother is waiting outside on his scooter.' Then she turned to Sarojini and said, 'I am leaving.' She dashed out from the kitchen.

Mani watched through the hall window as she left. Vanaja asked Sarojini, 'Who is that girl?'

'She is a classmate of mine.'

Amma asked Vanaja, 'You know Sundaram Iyer, don't you?'

'Which Sundaram Iyer?'

'Don't you remember, they lived next door when we were staying in that "two-taps" house? He was an assistant engineer? And his wife, that bulky mami with her lopsided gait?'

'So this is *that* Renuka? How she's grown!'

'Well, she is an adult now, isn't she? Must be twenty now, or even twentytwo.'

'No, Amma. She is not eighteen yet,' said Sarojini.

'That can't be. She must be at least three or four years older than you.'

When Sarojini came to the hall, Vanaja asked her, 'Isn't your friend wearing the end of her sari rather short?'

'Yes.'

'It's terrible to go around like that, showing off your entire back.'

'Almost all women wear it short these days. A lot shorter than that, in fact.'

'Why do they bother to wear a sari at all, then? What kind of fashion is this?'

Mani had changed into a full-sleeved shirt. He was rolling the cuffs up to his elbows as he came towards her. 'Saroja, tell Shankar when he comes here that he should go directly to Lakshmi Talkies.'

'Are you going to a movie?' asked Vanaja.

'Yes,' replied Mani, working up a painful grimace to put her off.

'Dei, dei, why don't you take me along?' pleaded Vanaja.

'No, absolutely not!' said Mani.

Vanaja moaned in self-pity, 'Only when I am here do I get to watch a few movies, or even go out. And when I ask you to take me, you act really annoyed.'

Mani's face continued to hold a scowl.

Vanaja quietly stepped out of his way. Her two older children were still sleeping, though it was not the time of day for children to be asleep. Their eighteen-hour train journey must have been really strenuous. Vanaja tried to wake them, 'Sudha, wake up. Dei, Balu, what's this, why are you still sleeping?'

Mani then said, 'If you don't bring your brood along, you can come with me.'

'Oh, I'm coming, I'm coming,' said an excited Vanaja. Sudha stirred a little. 'Go to sleep, go to sleep,' Vanaja urged her, gently patting her back.

'Hurry up, and be prepared to walk all the way when you come with me,' said Mani.

'It's only the end of the next street, da. Let me get ready. I'm going right now,' Vanaja assured him and rushed out. When she came back, some portions of her face were still not washed clean of soapsuds. She told Sarojini, 'Will you make some

Horlicks for Suresh at seven or seven thirty? You will find everything in that basket.'

Mani told Sarojini, 'Tell Shankar you don't know where I've gone.'

'Amma, I'm off to watch a movie with Mani,' Vanaja told her mother.

'You are going out for a movie immediately after you've arrived. Your father is not going to like it,' complained Amma.

'Never mind, Amma. Let me go today. Who knows if I'll be able to go some other time?' Vanaja took a silk sari out of her suitcase and began to get dressed. Though Mani paced impatiently near the gate in obvious foul temper, it was ten minutes before Vanaja was ready. 'Saroja, I'm leaving. Be sure to give the baby a little Horlicks. If he cries too much, give him this,' said Vanaja as she furtively squeezed the rubber nipple into Sarojini's palm, safely out of Mani's sight. Sarojini then happened to notice the end of her sister's sari. It was short all right.

•———•

Sarojini, taking advantage of the brief interval when she did not have Suresh underfoot, was writing in her lab record. She looked up, drew back her chair and offered it to the visitor. Then she went inside and informed her father, 'Appa, there is someone to see you.'

'Why don't you ask him to sit down?' said Appa.

'I have.'

Appa finished the second half of his shaving ritual in haste. Instead of wetting his half-dry shaving brush in the plastic shaving bowl, he dipped it in the sombu and lathered his face again, particularly the spot below the nostrils, and then the chin. Sarojini had fetched that sombu of hot water, hoping to at least wash her face after her father was done, because Vanaja was sure to shut herself up for long in the bathroom. Now it was wasted and he knew it. 'Saroja, throw this and get some well water,' he told her. But before Sarojini could do that, he had finished shaving. And in his clumsy haste, he toppled the plastic bowl. The stubble he had removed from his face with such strenuous effort floated in the ash-coloured soapy water, which was now beginning to flood the floor.

Sarojini made another trip to the bathroom to assess the situation. Vanaja was bathing her second child, Balu. It was hard to say which was louder—her threats and shouts at Balu, or his relentless bawling. Sarojini said, 'I'll have a quick bath as soon as you are through with him. It's a quarter past eight already.'

'Let me also have my bath. I'll only take a minute, and then you can go in. See, I've soaked all these clothes for washing.'

Sarojini grumbled to herself as she came back into the house. Her father and the visitor were talking on the veranda. That meant she could not even work on updating her lab record. Apart from the kitchen and the storeroom, the only place in that house with a roof overhead was the hall. All four corners of the hall were crowded with assorted bureaus and bedrolls stacked haphazardly along the wall. Another large item there was Mani's table. There was no room for Sarojini amidst this clutter. Suresh was doing his best to wax the floor with the lather from Appa's toppled shaving bowl. Sarojini told herself to let the mess be; nevertheless, she picked up Suresh and put him away somewhere safe. She then mopped the wet floor with a rag. Her father came in from the veranda and told her, 'Saroja, make a copy of your elder brother's horoscope and give it to me quickly.'

Saroja fetched her pen from her table on the veranda. Mani's horoscope had been cast very elaborately. Sarojini's horoscope was also in the same little notebook; in fact, all the children's horoscopes were written down there. But Mani's would take at least half an hour to copy—he was the firstborn male in the family. So her father, mother, and even the family astrologer must have been especially anxious about the time of his birth and the planetary configurations at that time.

Amma came from the kitchen and asked Appa who the visitor was. He gritted his teeth and said, 'I'll tell you later.' And went back to his conversation with the visitor.

Mani came back sweaty and breathless from his early morning exertions on the bicycle. Sarojini muttered 'Aiyo!' under her breath. Once he was back, he usually went to the bathroom and locked himself in. After his bath, he went to the kitchen, ate his brunch and left for work. In his hurry, he had neither the time nor the inclination to think of other people in the house, their needs, and the pressures on their time.

Appa called out to him, 'Mani, come here for a minute.' He joined them on the front veranda. Father and son were seldom on cordial terms and therefore, such easy familiarity between them was quite rare. But whenever an outsider was present, Appa took advantage of the situation and exercised a father's prerogative over his son, prudently, of course.

When Mani approached him, a little suspicious, Appa announced, 'This is my son.' Then he told Mani, 'Now you can carry on with your work.'

Mani lingered there for a moment puzzled, and then he came inside. Sarojini had just finished copying his horoscope. She rose to find some auspicious kungumam to mark the four corners of the sheet. 'What are you writing down?' Mani asked her. He knew for certain that it had something to do with him.

'Oh, it's your horoscope,' replied Sarojini.

'Bring it here. I am going to tear it up,' said Mani as he approached her threateningly. Sarojini ran to her mother for protection.

Amma asked Mani, 'You've just come in—what's the problem now?'

'Amma, Amma! It's Mani. He wants to tear up this copy!' complained Sarojini.

'Why do you behave like this?' Amma sighed.

'The way Appa treats me, why does he bother giving my horoscope to anyone?'

While this was going on, Appa came in flourishing a horoscope from the visitor. He asked Sarojini, 'Is it finished yet?'

'Here, Appa.' Sarojini gave him the copy.

The bathroom door opened slightly and Vanaja peeped out. 'Di, Saroja,' she shouted, 'close the hall door!'

As Sarojini left the kitchen to oblige her, Mani yelled at Vanaja, 'You've been here two months, and you still haven't learnt to close the door yourself?'

No one reacted to this outburst. Vanaja pulled a sour face as she marched to the storeroom to get dressed. Mani did not rush into the bathroom as Sarojini had expected him to. She picked up her sari, petticoat and other paraphernalia, and went in to bathe. As soon as she closed the door, she heard a child's voice call out, 'Chithi! Chithi!'

'Balu, go away! Let me have my bath.'

'But, Chithi...' whined Balu, squatting on the toilet. Without a word, Sarojini cleaned up Balu. She took no more than five minutes for her bath. Luckily for her, those five minutes passed without incident. Had there been a water tub near the well with a sombu beside it, people could have used the bathroom without too many interruptions. The others could then draw water from the well for their use. But Amma could not—she got chest pain immediately if she exerted herself. She had complained of acute pain even yesterday. Vanaja would not—she had her tubes tied up the day after Suresh was born, collecting thirty rupees from the government for her trouble. No matter what people from the sterilisation campaign claimed, her body had never been the same again. As for Muniyamma, she normally finished all her chores by eight and left.

Sarojini had to wear her sari inside the bathroom. She found that Appa was at the well. Within the next fortyfive minutes, he, along with Mani and Appu, must bathe, eat and leave for work. Appu had gone out with Sudha early that morning. He was not back yet.

Sarojini combed her hair once more to make it look tidy. She wore a pottu on her forehead. She collected her books for the day's classes at college. Then she went up to her mother. Amma was working with two stoves. Only the rice was ready. On one stove, kuzhambu was coming to a boil. On the other stove, Amma had placed a steel vessel into which she was dropping potatoes as she peeled them. Sarojini took her plate, and to speed things up, sat down beside her mother and joined her in peeling the potatoes. Balu was standing nearby and gawking hungrily at the potato roasting in the pan. 'Is she planning to put this boy and Sudha in school here?' Amma asked Sarojini.

'I don't know, Amma,' replied Sarojini.

'Didn't she ask your brother to find out about it yesterday?' Amma asked again.

'I don't know,' replied Sarojini. Amma was slicing the peeled potatoes in the vessel into small uniform pieces with the sharp edge of a flat ladle. To Sarojini, her face appeared to have grown dark, and her cheeks hung down worn and slack on both sides of her tired face. 'Let me eat whatever is ready. Or I'll miss the bus,' said Sarojini

'Sit down, then,' said Amma. 'Do you also want to eat now?' she asked Balu. He nodded.

Amma took a couple of ladles of kuzhambu which was not yet fully cooked, mixed it with a little mashed paruppu and served the concoction to Sarojini. The kuzhambu tasted far better than the fully cooked fare Sarojini usually ate. Vanaja was at the well, washing her children's clothes. Sarojini finished her meal and got up. Suresh was sitting on her table; he was busy tearing up her books. 'Anna, couldn't you have kept an eye on what he's been doing? You could have taken him down from the table!' she protested to Mani in a tearful voice.

'What? What is it?' He turned around, razor in hand.

Sarojini picked up Suresh and carried him straight to the well. 'What's the matter? Does he need washing up?' asked Vanaja.

'It seems as if that's all I get to do nowadays. He has torn up and ruined my books!'

'He is a child,' said Vanaja.

'If he is a child, why don't you keep him by your side and watch over him?'

'Who are you to tell me what to do in this house?'

Amma hurried over to them, asking, 'What is it now?'

Sarojini complained to her, 'Look at him, Amma. Suresh has torn up all my lab records!'

'Who is she to run things in this house?' screamed Vanaja. 'Who is she?'

'What has she done to you now?' Amma asked Vanaja.

'I didn't do or say anything, Amma. These are lab records, I have to keep them intact till my exams get over,' said Sarojini.

Mani came to the backyard to wash his razor, blade and shaving brush. For his part, he chipped in, 'I was going to ask you myself. Why don't you look after your children? They are yours, after all!'

'You can't even find a school to put them in, and now you're talking!'

'Vanaja, shut your mouth!' said Amma.

'If you fight with your husband and land up here whenever you please, which school will admit your children when they are closing for vacation?'

When Appa called out from the bathroom, 'What's the row about, now?' the fight dissolved by itself.

Amma wondered aloud, 'How come Sudha and Appu are still missing?' Sarojini gathered her books. Suresh had not ruined her books so grievously as to warrant such a fierce row. But Sarojini had not been aware of that when it started.

Although Sarojini was practically running to the bus stop, she tried to make it seem like a brisk walk. Thirty girls and forty boys were waiting there. Renuka was also there in this crowd. 'Didn't your brother give you a lift today?' Sarojini asked Renuka.

'His scooter needs to be repaired,' replied Renuka. 'Will you be there at the sabha programme next week?'

'How can I? I haven't fully revised a single subject yet,' said Sarojini. Then she asked, 'Whose programme is it going to be?'

'It's a dance concert by Kamala.'

'Perhaps my mother might want to go. She's been talking about going to Kamala's performance for quite some time.'

Sarojini got into the bus when it finally came. Since there were no seats vacant, she had to travel standing. As her bus was leaving the stop, she caught sight of Appu and Sudha as they got down from another bus.

•———•

'I was on my way to your house,' said the woman. She must have walked no more than twenty feet after getting off the bus, but she was already gasping for breath.

'Give me your bag. Let me carry it for you,' said Sarojini.

'Don't trouble yourself,' said the woman, but without much conviction. When Sarojini took hold of the bag's handle, she readily let go.

'After that day, your people didn't respond at all,' said the woman.

Sarojini walked on without attempting any reply.

'My husband has not been well these past two days. That's why I thought I'll make a visit myself and find out,' said the woman. 'What are they saying at your end?'

Sarojini pretended not to have heard this clearly. She asked, 'What was that?'

'They are happy about this proposal, aren't they?' The woman had rephrased her question this time.

'It's for the elders to give you a proper response, mami,' said Sarojini. They had reached her house by then. Sarojini opened the gate and knocked on the front door. The woman reclaimed her bag from Sarojini.

Vanaja opened the door. Though she was visibly surprised to see the woman, she said warmly, 'Come in, mami.' She led her into the hall and laid out a straw mat for her. Then she went to the kitchen, calling out to her mother.

Sarojini deposited her books on her table. Sudha was sitting under it. 'Why are you sitting there?' Sarojini asked her.

'I am waiting for Mama,' replied Sudha.

'So you'll be able to see him from there when he comes home? Come on out.' Sarojini pulled her by the hand.

Sudha came out on her own, saying, 'I'll come out myself, Chithi.' Sarojini passed the woman in the hall on her way to the kitchen. Amma came out just then, looking exhausted.

Vanaja asked Sarojini, 'So you've brought her here?'

'I didn't see her at all. She came up to me on her own and started talking. Looks like she was travelling in the same bus.'

Amma and Vanaja went to the hall. Sarojini quietly opened a few vessels in the kitchen and looked into them. She then went to the well. Balu, who was sitting on the stone used for washing clothes, came running to her, 'Chithi! Chithi!'

'How many times should I tell you not to fall all over my sari?' said an exasperated Sarojini. She caught hold of both his hands to ward him off, and not a moment too soon, it turned out. 'What have you done to yourself?' she asked him.

'Paati gave me groundnut sweet!' said Balu.

'Did you have to lick it so hard and get your face and hands sticky?' said Sarojini. It took more than half a bucket of water to clean him.

The tea had gone cold in the sombu. Sarojini poured herself some in a tumbler and drank it before going to the hall. At first glance, Amma and the woman seemed to bear a striking resemblance to each other.

'We are giving her away with only ten sovereigns, but don't let it trouble you. Why, next year we will have the valaikapu before the first delivery and the annual gift for the son-in-law, and so on. We will definitely make more gold jewellery for her—not less than five more sovereigns, let me tell you! She's a working girl. And if you feel she mustn't work after marriage, it is entirely up to you.'

'How much does she earn now?' asked Vanaja.

Speechless for a moment, the woman said in a slightly altered tone, 'Putting everything together, she brings home one hundred and ninety.' Amma was merely listening. Then the woman added. 'She always hands over her entire pay to us. She then draws money for her daily expenses out of that.'

A low crying sound could be heard from the other room. Immediately, Vanaja turned around. The whine grew into a loud bawl. Suresh crawled into the hall, clutching the rubber nipple in his small fist. His eyes were still drowsy from sleep. Amma said, 'Vanaja, go and look after the child.' Vanaja went to pick him up.

'Isn't he also your daughter's child?' asked the woman. 'You didn't bring him along when you came to see our girl, did you?'

'Yes, she had left him behind. Isn't there a limit to how many of us could trouble you?'

'Oh, that's all right. He is too young to be away from his mother.'

'She took care of him for a while,' said Amma, indicating Sarojini.

Then there was a loud noise, the front gate was being flung open. 'Anna has come,' Sarojini whispered to her mother.

The woman asked, 'Who?'

Mani parked his bicycle on the veranda. He took his shoes off and flung them to a corner. From where he was standing, it was not possible to see everyone in the hall. Mani had his shirt out of his trousers when he barged in there; he paled when he saw the visitor. He awkwardly marched through the hall to the back of the house. The moment the woman realised who he was, she was up and standing.

Amma said, 'Saroja, see what your brother wants.' Sarojini went inside.

Mani gnashed his teeth and snarled at Sarojini, 'Why couldn't you people warn me about the visitor?'

'Should we rush out and inform you as soon as you arrive?' Sarojini replied tartly.

Still angry, Mani ordered her, 'Go and bring my veshti from the coat stand.'

'Just imagine, if I go and bring your veshti in front of the visitor, what would she think of you?'

'Oh, all right, I'll get it myself' said Mani and marched into the hall. The woman was about to sit down just then—she sprang to attention again. When Mani took his veshti from the coat stand, a few other shirts and vests fell down. Mani did not pick them up. He came back to the kitchen.

Sarojini heated the tea for him. 'Isn't there any tiffin?' he asked her.

'I think Amma has made some sweets, but I don't know for sure,' said Sarojini.

From the hall, they could faintly hear the woman's pitch to Amma, 'If you could let me know soon, it would be of great help. My son lives in Shillong. He has to apply for leave well ahead if he wants to get here in time for the wedding. And he is the one who has to make all the arrangements. My husband has become quite feeble these days.'

Mani was quietly sipping his tea when Sudha came up to him, 'Mama...'

Mani told her sternly, 'Don't whine for no reason.' Sarojini compressed her lips. Frightened, Sudha was getting ready to cry. Mani said even more sternly, 'Ssshh!' Sudha's indignation vanished abruptly, she kept quiet.

Amma was saying, 'I'll ask my husband and let you know. He has sent both horoscopes to our village—'

'But you said they matched well when you had them examined here! We arranged for you to see our daughter only after you assured us of that!'

'But Appa always consults his chittappa in the village on such matters. My grandfather's younger brother has to see it and give his consent, only that will satisfy Appa,' said Vanaja.

Mani, overhearing this from the kitchen, sneered, 'As if she knows,' and resumed drinking his tea. After that, sounds of further conversation were few and faint. When Sarojini came to the hall after washing Mani's tumbler, the woman had already left.

Mani was at his table. He was making a lot of noise, picking up and dropping a number of things, ostensibly putting his table in order. 'What's the matter?' Amma asked him. Without answering her question, he picked up four or five old newspapers and flung them on the floor. 'What's with him?' Amma asked Sarojini.

'Didn't you prepare any tiffin today, Amma?'

'I was feeling very tired. I only made some groundnut sweet. Will you have a few pieces?' she asked Mani.

'I don't want anything.'

'I've prepared batter for idli tomorrow. Poor Vanaja, she has a small baby to look after, even so, she had to do the grinding. I'm feeling weak today, Mani,' she said.

Vanaja told her, 'Amma, start immediately if you want to go to the dance concert. It's getting late.'

'You don't feel too weak to go to the concert, but to make tiffin...' said Mani.

'You can go if you want to,' Amma told him.

'Amma, please go to the concert. If Mani goes, he won't sit there for even half an hour,' said Sarojini.

Amma went to the storeroom to change her sari. Mani asked them, 'Why are you people making them run around like this? You told them the horoscopes were all right, and now why do you have to say our uncle has to see them, or grandfather, or whoever?'

'Your father said that. Ask him tonight when he comes home, if you want to.'

'Then why did ten of us go to their place, ask all kinds of questions for two hours, eating bajji, sojji and all that?'

At this, everyone fell silent. Then, Amma spoke calmly from the storeroom, 'This won't be the only proposal you'll get. Maybe something more appealing will turn up later.'

'I don't know what on earth you would find appealing! Why, what's wrong with this girl?' Mani asked Vanaja. She remained silent. 'You went and saw her, didn't you? So tell us what you think.'

'How could I be the one to tell you? I am here today, and I will be gone tomorrow,' said Vanaja.

'Anna completely flipped for that girl when he saw her,' said Sarojini.

Mani gave her a murderous look. But her mother intervened in time, 'Dei, dei, leave her alone, will you? Somehow, I feel that this girl won't suit our family. I've said what I think, now do as you wish.' Mani took his cycle to the gate, he was still visibly agitated as he left for the evening.

Sarojini asked Vanaja, 'How *is* that girl?'

'Oh, she looks fine to me,' said Vanaja.

'Then?'

'I don't know. Amma has been saying right from the day we saw her that she won't suit us.'

Amma had changed into a fresh sari, but she still looked strange, as though something was wrong with her. 'Be sure to bring the season ticket back, Amma. There's one more concert this month,' said Sarojini.

At the gate, Amma turned around suddenly and said, 'Why don't you go, Vanaja? I'll stay home and look after the children.'

Sarojini pleaded, 'Amma, you've been talking about Kamala's dance all these days. If you'd like me to, I'll come along and drop you at the sabha.'

Amma and Sarojini walked to the bus stop. Amma said, 'I don't think I'll be able to walk from even the bus stop there to the sabha, di.'

'Shall we take a taxi, then? The fare's only eight annas, Amma.'

But as the taxi was approaching the sabha, Amma said, 'Sarojini, tell him to turn back. Something's happening to me, I feel so strange.' Amma was indeed perspiring a little more heavily than usual.

'Driver, take us back to where we started from,' said Sarojini.

Vanaja came rushing to the gate. 'What is it, Amma? What happened, Amma?' Vanaja asked her frantically. Amma raised her hand to tell her that she was all right, but she could not manage to speak.

Mani was not home yet. Appu never came home earlier than ten. Sarojini had to go to the doctor's clinic. There were five or six patients still waiting to see him. He said, 'Hello!' when he saw Sarojini.

Sarojini said, 'Amma.'

'Her blood pressure has shot up again? Just wait for ten minutes. I'll be with you as soon as I've seen these patients,' said the doctor. But it was fifteen minutes before the doctor was free. 'Let's go. Have you brought a vehicle?' he asked her.

'Shall I bring a taxi?' said Sarojini.

'If you are used to riding pillion on a scooter, you don't need to,' said the doctor. Sarojini did not say anything. The doctor brought the scooter out from his compound to the street. 'Your brother Appu brought her yesterday. I thought she was normal then. What happened?' asked the doctor.

'We had gone out for a while today. And then she had this pressure attack.'

'People like your mother shouldn't go out too often. Nor should they spend all their time in the kitchen,' said the doctor. 'Will you hold this bag and sit properly on the pillion? You won't feel scared?'

Sarojini sat on the pillion and held on tightly to the handgrip. At any rate, the doctor drove the scooter very slowly.

Her neighbours were standing at the entrance to her house—Sarojini could not understand why. When she reached the hall along with the doctor, they found Vanaja screaming. Vanaja's three children were also screaming with her. Amma no longer needed medical attention.

•———•

'You brainless oaf, why did you take down the poles before the planks are taken down?' The senior labourer was shouting at his junior. Immediately, the latter tried to tie the supports of the pandal back to the casuarina pole. There was a small pit near that pole, filled with slush and bits of darbai from the ceremonies.

Sarojini cried out, 'Don't hit him. Don't!' But the senior labourer had by then given the dullard a hard stinging slap. The younger man ran away, screaming abuses at his tormentor as he fled down the street. Though she could not understand the meaning of the terms, she knew that it was the kind of abuse that made your ears turn red.

Appa came around the house from the back and told her, 'Why don't you sit here after they've dismantled the pandal and taken it away?' After remaining unshaven for ten days through the ceremonies, Appa had removed his beard and moustache four days ago, but his face retained an unnatural sheen, as though he had shaved just yesterday.

Biting her trembling lower lip, Sarojini moved into the house with her books. The space on the veranda where her table used to be was now empty. They had erected a stone at that very spot to perform ceremonies for her dead mother. The pandal and the enclosure, which were erected for the ceremony, would be completely dismantled in a few minutes.

At the top of the stairs where the open terrace began, Appu and Mani were asleep on the floor. Sarojini was careful not to step on their sleeping bodies as she crossed over to a spot by the parapet wall; she crouched there and opened her book. They were sure to select some passages from this book for questions in her exam paper. This book, so familiar to her at other times, now read like it had been written in a strange, incomprehensible language.

Appu woke up suddenly. Mani's sleep was slightly disturbed by this sudden movement, but he turned over and went back to sleep. Appu asked Sarojini, 'What time is it?'

'Must be two, two thirty,' replied Sarojini. Half an inch of hair on Appu's forehead had been shaved off.

'Am...ma!' Appu yawned. 'What's going on downstairs?' he asked. 'What's all this noise?'

'They are taking the pandal apart,' replied Sarojini.

'Is there someone to oversee them?'

'Appa.'

Appu got up and went downstairs. Sarojini sat down with her knees drawn up in front of her. Then she too came downstairs, leaving her books behind. On the veranda, she found Vanaja talking in low whispers to her husband. He was listening to her intently, while quietly chewing betel leaf and areca nut. When his eyes fell on Sarojini, he asked her, 'Your exams begin tomorrow, don't they?'

'Hmm,' replied Sarojini.

'You poor thing.'

In the hall, a jumble of objects, large and small, lay in a corner. Sarojini's table was somewhere in that pile. On the other side, three mats were strewn on the floor. Suresh was asleep on one.

In the kitchen, Bhavani had lit the stove and kept some water on it for the afternoon coffee. Amma's older sister was also sitting there with her legs stretched out in front of her. 'Come to me, kannu,' she called to Sarojini. Sarojini went and sat down beside her. The next moment, she flung her arms around Periyamma and began to weep.

'Someone like me ought to have died first, but she's gone ahead and left me behind.' Periyamma grieved for her younger sister. It was many years since her husband had died, and she had no children.

Bhavani sobbed, 'I thought she would celebrate my valaikapu and I'd come and see her then. Now she's deceived me and gone away!' The water was boiling. Bhavani lifted the vessel off the stove and poured the hot water into the coffee filter. She then kept some more water on the stove.

'Does the milkman come around this time?'

'He's been coming as late as three thirty or four for the past few days. For all that, we haven't even asked for extra milk,' said Bhavani.

Periyamma stroked Sarojini's hair soothingly. Vanaja also came into the kitchen. Periyamma asked her, 'Isn't your husband planning to leave today?'

'I'm wondering whether I should also go back with him. Poor man, after eating out for two months at odd places he looks thin as a reed,' said Vanaja.

Periyamma said, 'You've been here for two months, why can't you stay for another ten days till Saroja's exams get over?'

'He said the same thing, Periyamma, but somehow I feel that I shouldn't leave him alone for any more. It's been long enough already,' said Vanaja.

Bhavani prepared coffee with milk left over from the morning. She poured some into a tumbler and said, 'Saroja, take this to Appa.'

Sarojini came out with the coffee tumbler. Her father was sitting on a chair in the same spot she had chosen earlier for its shade—the pandal had been up then. 'Has Vanaja's husband had his coffee?' he asked her.

'No, not yet,' said Sarojini.

'You could've served me after him and the others,' said Appa. When Sarojini did not respond, he took the tumbler from her. Appu and Vanaja's husband joined them. Appu had washed his face but he had not wiped it dry.

Vanaja's husband told Appa, 'I am planning to leave today.'

'Appu, move that bench down here,' said Appa. Vanaja's husband helped Appu shift the bench. He sat close to Appa. Appu went inside. Appa said in a voice already beginning to crack with grief, 'I don't know what I should do. I don't understand anything anymore.'

'Think now, if you, an elder, allow yourself to lose heart like this—what will a child like Sarojini do? You must be strong and courageous, especially now.'

'What kind of strength do I have left?'

Sarojini dashed inside very fast. But before she had had time to break down, Bhavani handed her another tumbler and said, 'Give this to your athimber. Here, this is for you.'

Sarojini came out again. By then, her father and Vanaja's husband had settled to normal everyday talk. Vanaja's husband said, 'Don't stop Sarojini's education for any reason whatsoever.

Let her at least earn a degree. If she is going to finish her pre-university course and remain at home, she could have stopped with her SSLC. So, let her study further.'

Sarojini gave him his coffee. Sudha came in from the neighbour's house, leading Balu by the hand. Balu was holding his wet underwear in his hand. Vanaja, who had somehow managed to see him from inside the house, came out immediately and took him away. Vanaja's husband told Sarojini, 'Look here, Saroji, you mustn't keep weeping. You have a lot to do in life, you must be strong. You must do well in your exams, study further, and look after your father and brothers. I've asked your sister to stay back here for a month to help you, but remember—you are in charge of this house now.'

Sarojini went back to the kitchen with the empty coffee tumblers. Vanaja's children were eating curd rice. Bhavani and Vanaja sat in front of them, talking. Appu was sitting next to Periyamma, listening. Periyamma said, 'Why are you people in such a hurry? Saroja is yet to be married—your mother would have planned to give most of her jewellery for her wedding. If you want to take it all away, what are we to do when that child gets married? Somehow, I don't feel this is right.'

Bhavani said in a weepy voice, 'Amma was saying she would definitely make a pair of sugarcane bangles for my valaikapu.'

'Sugarcane notch bangle?' asked Vanaja.

Bhavani sat silent for a moment. Then she said, 'Yes, sugarcane notch bangle.' She did not cry this time.

Suresh, who woke up just then, came there looking for his mother, bawling. Vanaja shouted at him, 'Why didn't you sleep for some more time? Are you in such a hurry?' Then he cried even louder.

Periyamma said, 'There's one more girl left to be married. And the boys are single too. It is not right to divide the jewellery and take away everything now.'

By then, Mani also woke up and came in. Everyone fell silent when they saw him. He said, 'I have to go to work from tomorrow. So, see to it that the cooking is finished early—not delayed like today.'

Appu also said for his part, 'My leave gets over today.'

Bhavani gave Mani his tumbler of coffee. His face had darkened. Like Appu, his forehead was also shaved in the front. Periyamma told Mani, 'Try not to go out of town for at least a year. You have to make sure that you perform all the monthly ceremonies for your mother.'

Mani listened without reacting. Then he asked Sarojini, 'If you have an exam tomorrow, why don't you go look at your books? What are you doing here?'

'Mani, why are you always after this child? She's just come here. Poor thing, she can't even find a place to sit and study, this house is so crowded,' said Periyamma.

'What can I do about it? Anyway, I am going to put her table back in its place.' Then Mani turned to Bhavani and said, 'How about you? Do you have to go home, or are you staying here till after your delivery? It would be better if you people discuss and decide whatever you want when Periyamma is still here.'

'What can she decide on her own, the poor thing? Doesn't she have to consult her father? And ask her in-laws?' said Periyamma.

'That's why I said she should consult everyone while they are still here. Just making sure what happened to me doesn't happen to her. There's no reason why it should, is there?' said Mani, as he got up to leave.

'What does he mean?' asked Periyamma.

'Anna feels very sad that he wasn't present at Amma's side when she died.'

'When she was alive, there wasn't a single day when he didn't snarl at her,' said Vanaja.

'Why rake up all that now?' said Appu. 'What are you making for tiffin? I am really hungry,' he said.

Bhavani told Vanaja, 'If we had some ravai, we could make uppuma.' Vanaja had started preparing milk for Suresh.

Periyamma got up and slowly moved towards the well. Sarojini followed her there. 'Periyamma!' she called softly.

'What is it, kannu?' asked Periyamma. Then suddenly, she said, 'Chee! You foolish girl. You mustn't keep crying, thinking of your mother. You have your father. Your brothers. Your sisters. You have all these people, and I am here for you. You mustn't weep all the time.'

'Somehow Periyamma, I feel very scared.'

Periyamma held Sarojini in a tight embrace, stroking her head and her back. 'Whatever has happened, has happened. You have to look after your father from now,' she said. 'In ten, or at the most twenty days, Vanaja would have gone back home. Bhavani will also go home after her delivery. More than any of you, your father's going to have a very difficult time. You must take special care of him.'

Sarojini asked, 'Won't you have to stay alone when you get back, Periyamma? Why don't you come here and stay with us? Won't you be a mother to us, now that our mother is no more?'

Periyamma stood still for a moment as though astonished by Sarojini's plea. 'How can I come and stay here, amma? I have four tenants living in my house. How can I leave everything unattended, and come to live here? Soon, when Mani gets married, there will be a woman in this house. Where's the need for me, then?'

Sarojini left her there and came to the veranda. Her table was back in its place below the staircase. Appa was still sitting in the open. In the hall, Appu was showing Sudha how to skip without letting the rope hit the floor. Vanaja's husband was keeping an eye on them as he pulled and fastened the straps of his 'hold-all' for the night's journey.

Determined to study, Sarojini sat down at her table.

•———•

Sarojini prepared the sambar rice and curd rice in separate containers; she then took the milk off the stove. Despite her instinct telling her that she shouldn't put out the coal fire by sprinkling water, she nevertheless sprinkled water on the burning red hot embers, which contracted, emitted smoke and went out, forming a nascent coat of ash. She needed four tablespoons of milk to make a tumbler of coffee with the decoction she had. After pouring the coffee into a flask and putting it away, she went to the front door, peeped out and came back to the kitchen. Five minutes later, Appu came home from work. She took the empty tiffin-carrier from him, and rinsed it in a great hurry. After transferring the sambar rice and curd rice into separate compartments in the tiffin-carrier, she wiped the outer surface clean with a kitchen rag. Appu was still sitting on a chair into which he'd settled the moment he'd arrived. Sarojini gave him the two bags, 'Here, food and coffee.'

'Nothing for me?' asked Appu.

Sarojini bit her tongue and said, 'I'll make you coffee.'

'Don't bother. I'll make it myself. Why don't you go to the hospital today in my place? Just today?' said Appu.

'Why are you telling me this so late? If I try to get ready and leave now, it will be past six by the time I reach the hospital!'

'Please, can't you go today? Whenever I visit, she keeps ordering me around saying, "ask the doctor", "tell the RMO", and so on.'

'I simply can't go there now, all of a sudden!'

'Then I am not going there, either. Let none of us go to the hospital today.'

Sarojini rushed to the kitchen. A minute later, she went to the storeroom, picked up a sari and got dressed. Appu had not moved from his chair. 'All right, I am going. Watch out for the cat, or it'll drink the milk. Where is the pass?' Appu took out a crumpled and worn piece of paper and gave it to her.

Sarojini found some other woman in Bhavani's bed in Ward 9. Sarojini asked her, 'Where is my sister?' Though the woman's eyes were open, she didn't appear to have registered Sarojini's question.

Sarojini went looking for the nurse in charge of the ward. In the matron's office, she found a nurse, who was busy looking for something. She yelled at Sarojini, 'Why did you come here? Go. Go away. Get out. Do you think this is a private nursing home that you can wander around? Go away, visiting hours are over and they've rung the bell.'

'Where is Bhavani who was in Bed 13? I came to see her,' said Sarojini.

'Is she a "primie"?' asked the nurse.

A second later, Sarojini replied, 'Yes, this is her first delivery.'

'Oh, her pains stopped, and she was shifted to Ward 4 in the afternoon,' said the nurse.

'Where is Ward 4?' asked Sarojini.

'Why don't you people come at the proper time? Go downstairs, it's near the operation theatre,' replied the nurse.

Before Sarojini could reach Ward 4, they had rung the second bell—all visitors were trooping out. A fat woman was coming down the ward, pushing a trolley whose wheels squeaked for want of grease. Two others were distributing milk and bread from the trolley to the patients. Bhavani was in tears. 'Have some coffee first,' said Sarojini.

Bhavani wiped her eyes and asked Sarojini, 'Why did you take so long?'

'I couldn't get a bus on time. Also, I didn't know they'd shifted you to another ward,' replied Sarojini.

'Any letters?'

'No.'

Bhavani looked even more disappointed. She took the coffee and had a sip. 'Didn't you add any sugar?'

'But I did!'

'Try some yourself,' said Bhavani.

Sarojini opened the low cupboard next to Bhavani's bed and looked inside. The sugar bottle they had brought from home was empty. Sarojini then said, 'I have made the rice quite soft today, just as you wanted.'

'Leave the food over there,' said Bhavani. Then she said, 'Have you brought the sari, bodice and petticoat I had asked for?'

'You'd asked for them?'

'You haven't brought anything? I sent word through Appu. Didn't he tell you?'

'Why, no!'

Bhavani began weeping again. The ward nurse called out to her, 'Who's there? Why are you still standing here? How many times do I have to tell you to clear out? You go out one way, sneak back through another and hang around here? Don't you have any sense?'

'I have just come in, sister. I'll leave now,' said Sarojini. Turning to Bhavani, she said, 'I'll send everything tomorrow morning along with the coffee. Tell me, what else do you need?'

'Let me go to hell any which way! Why should anybody care?' Bhavani cried some more.

'Tell me what you need. How can I send you anything unless you tell me?'

Bhavani wiped her eyes.

'Why get angry with you?' she said. 'I had kept a pair of white saris in the cardboard carton. Send me one of those. The white sari, and then the bodice, petticoat and blouse that

I'd sent home yesterday for washing—send these four things, will you?'

'You're out of sugar, aren't you?'

'Yes. Sugar, Horlicks.... Ask Appa to come here tomorrow. If I don't deliver by morning, I can at least go home. No doctor will give me a proper reply.'

'Should I ask them now?'

'You...? All right, find out and come back.'

Sarojini hesitated, not knowing which way to go. Bhavani said, 'The RMO and the others, none of them will be available now. If you don't catch them before ten or ten thirty in the morning, they will be available only after seven in the evening.'

'Let me try and find out.' Sarojini walked down the corridor.

In a small room, she chanced upon two nurses checking items from the hospital's laundry and putting them away into the cupboards. One of them saw Sarojini and said, 'Ei, who are you? Go, go away. Matron will be here any moment now.'

Sarojini said, 'One minute, sister.'

The nurse stopped her work to ask, 'What is it?'

'My sister is in Ward 4. Who should I ask whether they are going to discharge her tomorrow?'

'Which ward?'

'Ward number 4.'

'Oh, that's the case which was shifted this afternoon,' said the other nurse.

'It's been ten days since she was admitted here—' Sarojini began.

'False pains. But it's the right time. She might go into labour any moment now.'

'Can't I see a doctor?'

'Number seven is Doctor Janamma's case. She has out-patient duty tomorrow, she may come in as late as eleven. If there are any adults at home, ask them to come here at lunchtime. They can ask the doctor then. Send your mother tomorrow.'

'But we have no mother. She is no more.'

'Then send some other grown-up person.'

'There's only my father....'

'Send a woman.'

Sarojini came back to Bhavani. By then, they had turned on the lights in that room. 'Did you find out anything?' asked Bhavani.

'I'll come again tomorrow morning,' said Sarojini. A clipboard with many sheets of paper on it was hanging by a short length of cord from the foot of Bhavani's bed. If she managed to sneak a look, she might get to learn something, however half-baked, about Bhavani's condition.

Sarojini saw out of the corner of her eye that a nurse in the ward was staring fixedly at her. Bhavani said, 'Go now. If you linger, that nurse is going to take it out on me after you leave.'

As Sarojini was about to leave, Bhavani asked, 'Did anybody go and look up Periyamma? When did she say she was coming?'

'Appa himself went to see her. She told him she would come and stay with us after the delivery.'

All the normal exit routes from the wards to the hospital gate were closed by then. Sarojini had to walk through several blocks and visit the casualty ward before she could find her way out. She missed two buses because there was no room, and boarded the third after suffering some pushing and jostling. Instead of going home directly, she went to Renuka's house. Renuka seemed somewhat restless.

'Found out anything?' asked Sarojini.

'My brother left just now. I believe that man called to say that he would definitely have the information today. I am scared, Saroji. Stay with me, di.'

Renuka's mother said, 'Oh, are you coming from the hospital? Could you keep your bag outside, over there?'

Then, 'Your mother's ceremonies are going on all right, aren't they?'

Sarojini replied, 'Mmm...'

'She was such a helpful woman. Now she's deceived us all and gone away, all of sudden.' Renuka's mother's voice choked with suppressed tears. Then she asked, 'Are you people going to celebrate your sister's seemantham?'

'I believe we can do it even after the delivery. Her mother-in-law has written to say that we can celebrate it along with the naming ceremony,' said Sarojini.

'First child—what a pity the grandmother won't be there to prepare the mother's diet and to give oil baths to her grandchild.'

Renuka's brother arrived. He had advance information on the results of the pre-university exams through an acquaintance in the University's administrative office. Renuka had given him a piece of paper with six or seven registration numbers scribbled on it. He had brought back that piece of paper. Sarojini's number was also on it. Against her number were the words—First Class.

•———•

Appa was reading the day's newspaper. Sarojini got down from the ricksha and took the baby from Bhavani. When the baby's face was exposed to direct sunlight for a fleeting moment, it whimpered—though its eyes were tightly shut—and kicked its legs. Bhavani got down and walked with feeble steps past the gate into the house.

Sarojini told the ricksha-driver, 'Wait here for a minute. I'll be back,' and followed Bhavani.

Appa asked Bhavani, 'What happened?' Bhavani went in as though she had not heard anything.

Sarojini said, 'The doctor has asked us to stop the old medication. He's prescribed some new medicines. He's said that the baby should not be breastfed.'

'What can you give a twenty-day-old baby except breastmilk?' asked Appa.

Sarojini did not say anything. She went inside and laid the baby on the floor. Then she went to the kitchen, took the rice off the stove and put the rasam to boil. She went to the storeroom, and among the many boxes there, picked a small wooden case, opened it and took out a peppermint tin and shook it slightly. The box had always been heavy with coins when her mother was alive, but now it was empty.

Sarojini came to the veranda and told her father, 'Appa, I need seventyfive paise.'

'Look in my coat pocket,' said Appa. She found only a lot of loose papers in Appa's coat pocket.

'What are you looking for?' asked Bhavani.

'Nothing,' replied Sarojini.

The change in Appa's coat pocket added up to less than half a rupee. Sarojini went to the ricksha-driver and gave him the change, saying, 'Look, come back here after your school trip. I'll give you the rest.'

Bhavani said, 'Sometimes, we don't have enough money even to pay for the ricksha.'

Appa told Sarojini, 'You could have asked Mani if he had some change.'

Sarojini replied, 'Anna is in the bathroom.'

Appa folded the newspaper and put it down. He went inside and asked Bhavani, 'What did the doctor say?'

Bhavani replied in a normal tone, 'He has asked us to give the medication. We can give the child only dilute arrowroot porridge and water mixed with glucose for the next two days.'

'Do we have arrowroot flour in the house?' asked Appa

'No,' said Sarojini.

Appa said, 'I'll go and get some immediately.'

Sarojini went to the kitchen. Appa had put his shirt on and was about to leave when the sastrigal arrived. 'What is it?' said Appa.

'Tomorrow and the day after,' said the sastrigal.

Mani came in, fresh from his bath. He had grown dark and thin. He also asked the sastrigal, 'What is it?'

'Tomorrow and the day after. I'll send the old man nice and early tomorrow.'

Mani looked at his father. 'Isn't it the day after and the day after that?' Appa asked the sastrigal.

'No. You've reckoned the dates by the calendar here. It has everything printed wrong this month,' said the sastrigal.

'Oh, god!' exclaimed Mani.

'Why? What's the matter?' asked the sastrigal.

'Had I known this earlier, I would have shaved today. The commissioner and under secretary and everyone else arrived from Delhi this morning. For the next four days, I have to present myself with stubble on my face.'

The sastrigal seemed to think that his responsibilities were over. He asked Bhavani, 'Bhavani, are you all right? Everything's fine?'

'Why don't you shave today? Then it'll be all right,' Appa told Mani.

'But I've had my wretched bath already,' grumbled Mani.

'So what?'

The sastrigal again looked at his watch. 'I'll send the old man exactly at eight thirty. You can finish everything by ten and reach your office on time,' he told Mani.

'Hmm, let's see,' said Mani. In the kitchen, Sarojini took the boiling rasam off the stove. Now she had to garnish the vegetable and roast it lightly. But she did not do it right then.

The sastrigal turned a little towards the kitchen. 'Listen, Saroja, go and bring your periyamma home today.'

Mani said, 'I'll go and inform her.'

Saroja now poured a little oil into the frying pan.

'So, I'll be leaving then?' The sastrigal started out.

'All right,' said Appa.

On his way out, the sastrigal stopped and turned. 'It looks like you haven't sent any word to Krishnaswamy Iyer.'

Sarojini knew at once who Krishnaswamy Iyer was. Mani knew too, but strangely, he was not annoyed.

'Who? Which Krishnaswamy Iyer?' asked Appa.

'That retired railway auditor. You remember—all of you went and saw that girl when Mani's mother was alive. Mani, should you delay these things further? Don't you see how difficult it becomes when you keep delaying things? If you decide quickly, we can fix a date even as early as August. Only if you are married will you get the full benefit from all these ceremonies you are performing for your mother.'

Mani stood there listening. Appa said, 'I'll let you know.'

The sastrigal said, 'Good lineage, good family. They'll spend eight or ten thousand just for gold ornaments.'

'Poor Amma, she's gone,' said Bhavani.

'A pity, that's true. She could have lived for another twenty years. She's passed away well ahead of her time.... But the rest of us have to get on with our lives. And everything has to happen at the proper time, don't you agree? After you, Mani, there is Appu, and then there is Saroja. See how it's all held up, waiting for you to make up your mind!

'Where is Appu? Please tell him about the ceremony. It would be enough if he takes the forenoon off, the day after tomorrow. Tomorrow, he can finish everything by ten and leave for work.'

Appa asked Sarojini, 'Can you manage a little coffee?'

'No, I don't want any. It's more than six months since I gave up coffee. No, don't bother, Saroja.' Then the sastrigal turned to her father, 'What happened to Saroja's medical college application?'

'Well, she has applied. We'll have to see what happens.'

'She's got a first class, hasn't she?'

'Oh yes, first class, distinction in one subject....' Appa pulled out his sacred thread and showed it dramatically to the sastrigal. 'Even if you earn distinction in three subjects, they'll say "no" if you have this. Won't be easy with a single "D", I should think.'

'I'll be leaving, then. Mani, tell Appu to stay here with you tomorrow. I never get to see him when I come.' The sastrigal left.

Appa went to the veranda and called out, 'Mani.' Mani went up to him. Sarojini moved from the kitchen to the veranda. Appa asked Mani, 'Can you spare two rupees? We need to buy some provisions for the house.'

Mani went in without a word, took a ten rupee note from his wallet and gave it to his father. 'You can also buy vegetables for tomorrow and the day after,' he suggested.

'Can't do it now. I'll just buy a tin of arrowroot powder and little oil. We can attend to the rest this evening,' said Appa.

Sarojini said, 'Appa, I have to go to my college today.'

'Bhavani will be left alone, Sarojini. Why don't you go after Periyamma gets here?'

'If you can't get me a seat in medical college, I must see if I can get admission in a BSc course at least. If I don't do it now, nothing will be available later.'

'They'll want three thousand and four thousand, amma. Where will I go for that kind of money?'

'Then why did we apply to medical college for admission? If we can't afford it, we needn't have bothered at all!'

Appa asked Mani, 'Did Appu give his salary this month?'

Mani said, 'I never ask him anything. He hasn't been giving money for two or three months now.'

'What is he up to?'

'When *you* haven't asked him, how can I?'

'Earlier, he used to come home late at night. Now he goes away first thing in the morning.'

Sarojini went inside, keeping well out of this conversation. Bhavani asked her, 'Have you finished cooking?'

'Yes. You can eat with Appa. He'll be here any minute.'

'Why BSc and all that bother? I pleaded so much, but Appa and Anna simply refused to send me to college.'

'Well, they were trying to get you married at that time.'

The baby stirred a little, and started crying. '*Tho, tho, tho...*' Bhavani tried to pacify it by patting it gently on the back. Sarojini also knelt beside her and removed the baby's sheet. The baby had wet itself. Mani peeped in and then moved away to the veranda.

Appu came in then. He too had grown thin and dark. Bhavani asked him, 'Have you had your bath?'

'Yes,' replied Appu.

'Don't you give any money for the household expenses?'

'How does that concern you?'

Sarojini said, 'Appa mentioned it for the first time today.'

'To whom?'

'To Anna.'

'Is he such a gem of a son—that fellow?'

'Are you talking about me?' Mani asked as he came in.

'Nothing that should concern you,' replied Appu.

'Listen, fight as much as you want to after I leave. Don't have these rows while I am still here,' said Bhavani. Appu knelt down and started playing with the baby. She continued, 'Why don't you change into a veshti? The three of us can eat together. Sarojini has to go to her college today.'

Appu said, 'Oh, all right.'

As he said that, their father came in with the arrowroot tin and oil. Appu stood up when he saw his father.

Appa went past him into the kitchen and laid out his purchases on the floor. When he came back to the hall, he said to no one in particular, 'Ceremonies for your mother are to be performed tomorrow and the day after. So try and stay home in the morning.'

Appu paused for a minute before he spoke, 'Appa, there is something I want to tell you.' He paused again and said, 'I am going to get married.'

'Oh, good! We are trying to find a bride for your elder brother, and you want to race ahead? Wonderful!'

Appu did not reply.

'We have one more girl in this house yet to be married. Don't do anything that'll make us hang our heads down in shame.' Appu did not speak. Appa spoke as though he had suddenly recalled something, 'Oho, is that why you have been saving up your salary? Very good, very good!'

'So, when is the wedding?'

'Tomorrow.'

'But tomorrow is the ritual for your dead mother!'

Appu did not reply.

Appa had a final question, 'At least, is the girl a brahmin?'

'No.'

No one spoke after that.

•———•

Sarojini felt that if her face had a little more vitality in it, that man from Mohan Photo Studio might not have dared to make that obscene gesture at her. Not just her face—her limbs; her hair, untended and in permanent disarray; her crumpled and worn sari; her daily trips to the provision store next to his studio in this shabby state to buy this and that; and the day she dropped a packet of salt on the street in front of his studio and had to leave in acute embarrassment with the salt scattered on the mud—all this too must have emboldened him, thought Sarojini. Even though his photo studio was barely bigger than those bunk stores which sold paan, beedis and cigarettes, he brazenly leered at her with his mouth wide open in a mocking grin—his stained teeth repulsive, with those large gaps in between.

As she passed the bus stop, Sarojini got off the pavement and stood on the road waiting to cross to the other side, though she did not really need to. Before the cycle ricksha which was coming down the road at an unpredictable speed could clear out of her path, Renuka had spotted her. She called out, 'Saro!' Sarojini turned and smiled at her.

'Why are you going away as though you hadn't seen me?'

Sarojini merely stood there, protracting her dutiful smile.

'Are you in a great hurry?' asked Renuka.

'Why don't you come home with me?' said Sarojini.

'I came to your place on Sunday morning and waited for you for more than half an hour. You never turned up.'

'I had gone to buy milk coupons on Sunday morning.'

'I didn't know where you'd gone, but you weren't back till ten o' clock.'

'If you'd ever bought milk coupons, you would know how long it takes normally.'

'Why do you have to stand in the queue for milk coupons? Why can't your father or brother do that?'

Sarojini asked her, 'Has Miss Premavathy resigned yet?'

For a moment, it seemed as though Renuka did not know what to say. Then she said, 'Do you really want to know? Aren't you simply trying to change the subject?'

'Why, can't I ask you about your college?'

'What can I tell you? It's a real scandal. Even while you were there, she had been visiting seedy lodges and places like that. Meanwhile, she filed a false complaint against the hostel cook and got him suspended. Now it's her turn to pay for her sins. Why don't you come to the college sometime?'

'Sure. I will.'

'Of the seventeen girls in our batch, ten are doing BSc Chemistry.'

'I know.'

'Janu dropped out in the first year itself. Only you didn't join us, you kept talking grandly of MBBS.'

'Anyone who takes biology group subjects in pre-university is sure to dream of becoming a doctor.'

Then suddenly, Sarojini felt her face darken with humiliation. That man from Mohan Photo Studio was walking past. Because of the teeming crowd at the bus stand, he couldn't even be blamed for bumping into them as he passed. 'I'll be near Sundaram Park at six o' clock.' He said this slowly and clearly and continued walking.

Renuka watched him go without any sign of perturbation. She then asked Sarojini, 'Isn't he the photographer?'

Sarojini asked her, 'Do you know him?'

'A perfect match for Miss Premavathy,' said Renuka.

'There is not even a single new photograph in his studio—only old faded ones.'

'But he always keeps showing his teeth to all the girls.'

'I must go now, Renuka. I must stop on the way and leave word at the charcoal depot to send us a sack of coal.'

'Why can't your brother get married soon?'

'People used to send proposals earlier, but he kept saying no. Now, hardly anyone approaches us with a horoscope.'

'Can I say something, if you promise not to get upset?'

'What is it? Tell me quickly, I must leave.'

'At least your second brother has married someone and settled down. Your eldest brother doesn't seem to have the guts to do that.'

Sarojini did not respond at all.

Renuka continued, 'He keeps putting it off because he is scared of the responsibility.'

'At least, he lives at home with us.'

'Why wouldn't he? You are living there too—just to cook and feed him three times a day!'

Renuka then got into a bus and left. Sarojini came home with the provisions. She spent some time putting away everything. Appa was rinsing the vessels washed by Muniyamma that morning, and placing them upside down on the kitchen ledge to drain the water.

'Why don't you serve us food? It is getting late,' he told her.

'So what if it's getting late?' asked Sarojini.

Appa raised his head and looked at her. 'I'll retire in another month. You wouldn't have to do things in a hurry after that.'

Sarojini took a handful of cooked rice from the pot and went to the well and kept it there in the open for the crows to feed. Only then did she realise that she had forgotten the ritual of offering food to the gods on the puja shelf. She let it pass, and placed Appa's plate at its usual spot on the kitchen floor. Hearing the sound of vessels, Mani got up from his perch near the stairs and went to the backyard. When his father was ready to eat, Mani came and sat down next to him. He was wearing a filthy veshti. Appa looked at him and then fixed his gaze down on his plate. Sarojini asked Mani, 'Have you had your bath?'

Mani clucked his tongue.

Sarojini served them rice. Appa said, 'We are out of washing powder. Muniyamma has asked us to get some.'

'Do I have to worry about even things like washing powder and promptly buy it when we've run out? Why can't one of you do that?'

Mani continued eating his food without a word. Appa said in humble appeasement, 'I'll do it, definitely I will.'

'From now on, don't expect me even to go in the direction of the provision store,' said Sarojini.

'All right, all right!' said Appa, as he continued eating.

For a moment, her father and brother seemed like inert dolls to Sarojini—dolls, which could do no more than shake their limbs mechanically. What good were they to anyone?

Mani went to work wearing the same filthy veshti. Sarojini latched the front door and sat down to eat. The food was bland that day, she had completely forgotten to add salt. Appa and Mani had eaten it without uttering a word. Sarojini locked the back door too before she spread a mat on the floor and lay down. The mat had been purchased just a few days before her mother's death. Now the edges were frayed, and the straw was unravelling. Except for the day's sheet on the daily calendar, everything in that house appeared old and worn out.

Sarojini picked up a couple of weekly magazines and lay down again on the mat. Even the stories in those magazines were old. At noon, the postman came with a letter. She recognised Vanaja's handwriting on the envelope.

We are fine here. Are you all doing well? It's raining here. Is it raining over there? Sudha and Balu are doing well at school. Has Mani agreed to any proposal? My namaskarams to Appa.

She would have written something on those lines. Sarojini left the envelope unopened on the table. Then she opened it and had a look. Vanaja's letter contained only one unusual item: *I have been told that Appu has had a daughter. Have you been to see the baby yet?*

Muniyamma, who arrived for her afternoon chores, asked her, 'What, kannu, no coffee tumbler today?'

'No. I didn't make coffee this afternoon.'

'Why are you moping about the house all alone?'

'Well, someone has to stay back in every house.'

'The way you are living, kannu, it's not good for you.'

'Why don't you mind your own business?'

'How can I let you remain like this? Why don't you at least get your periyamma to come and stay here with you, kannu?'

'But she doesn't want to stay here, Muniyamma.'

'All right, give me some washing powder.'

'We don't have any. Do your washing without the powder.'

Muniyamma muttered something to herself as she went about her chores. After she had swept and mopped the floor, she started out with an empty bottle and milk coupon to fetch milk. 'Should I get anything for you from the hotel, kannu?' she asked Sarojini.

'I don't need anything.'

'Do what you want, then,' said Muniyamma and left.

Sarojini arranged the washed vessels on the kitchen shelves. Then she stood in front of the mirror and looked at herself. Nobody could mistake it for a child's face anymore. She went back to the kitchen and checked—the rice and kuzhambu would do for the night. There was also a lot of leftover rice soaking in a large vessel.

Sarojini started cleaning the house. Muniyamma who returned with the milk bottle protested, 'What is this? You are bringing down all that dirt and cobwebs now, just after I've swept the floor! I can't sweep again.'

'I'll do it myself, Muniyamma. You can leave,' said Sarojini.

She cleaned the shelves and cupboards which had not been cleaned for months. Then she moved the trunks and boxes from their positions along the wall and cleaned out the dirt and rubbish from the nooks and corners. She found many objects that had been given up as lost—comb, key ring, a lone glass bangle, a napkin stitched for Bhavani's child, baby rags, Appu's vest. After she had finished sweeping, Sarojini wiped the pictures on the wall, and the calendars. The portrait photograph of her parents, from the time before Sarojini was born, had acquired a sepia tint and was now being eaten up by termites. Amma sat stiffly, wearing a blouse with sleeves that came down below her elbows. She could see the stiffness in her mother's posture. But her father had been inert as a doll even all those years ago.

She cleaned the framed pictures of gods on the puja shelf and also the miniature metal icons. Only two sombus filled with water from the holy Ganga were left. The big copper one, which had been badly dented over the years, had been broken to anoint her mother's corpse. After that, no one thought about water from the Ganga. Appu's pendant with a portrait of Saibaba was lying there. He had forgotten that he had kept it there when he turned the house upside down looking for it—now he may have forgotten Saibaba himself. Sarojini wanted to see Appu. He had become the father of a child. But he was not concerned about them at all. Neither did they bother about him. Only Vanaja wrote to him now and then.

Mani returned from work. At first, Sarojini did not move. Then she went to make coffee. Mani went straight to the backyard. When he came back, he picked up an old spy thriller and sat down in the hall to read it, leaning his back against the wall. When Sarojini gave him coffee, he drank it, after which he reached out to the coat stand for his shirt—he was going out. Sarojini said, 'Don't you go off anywhere. I have to go out this evening.'

'Are you going out to buy vegetables or something?' asked Mani.

'Should I go out only to slave for you people?'

Mani hung his shirt back on the coat stand and leaned his back on the wall as before, going back to his spy thriller.

When Sarojini left the house after running a comb through her hair to give it a semblance of neatness, her father had not arrived yet. At any rate, he would be back home in half an hour, or an hour at the most.

Sarojini told herself over and over again that she was not being reckless. She went straight, turned left and then walked straight again, before she turned right and crossed the playground. It was so close to where she was going that the cones of the asoka trees were already visible. When she crossed the playground and turned left, there was Sundaram Park on the other side of the street.

Malati

Attending Sashi's wedding had been a mistake. Had she kept away, perhaps this whole business about the doctor wouldn't have turned so serious.

Earlier, Malati had decided she couldn't go. 'You go ahead and attend the muhurtam. I'll attend the reception if I can,' she had told her mother.

'How can you say that? Everyone in her family had come to invite us. You studied with her up to SSLC. They've come home for every single occasion, good and bad. People will talk if you don't go to her wedding.' Amma was cross with her.

'Amma, I don't get a moment to spare at the nursing home till ten o'clock. The clerk has been on leave for ten days, and the doctor's warned me a few times already.'

'Is your job so important that you can't even attend a friend's wedding? Does that doctor pay you so much money?'

'Whether he pays much or not, he is the only one who pays promptly on the first of every month. Why don't you tell me if you want me to lose this job too? I'll then be free to attend everybody's wedding and seemantham with you.'

'I wouldn't know about that. That child had come here and personally invited you. If I go there without you, it won't look all right. People will say you didn't come because you are envious.'

'I don't feel envious about anybody.' Malati was close to tears now.

'Cry, then. In this birth, it's my fate to weep with you all my life.'

As a result of this row, the quantity of leftover rice Malati usually had every morning was much reduced that day. She began to feel hungry soon after she reached the nursing home.

At least five of the eight patients who were admitted in that nine-bed nursing home would have said, 'I don't feel hungry at all.' However, once a patient was admitted to a private nursing home, his or her entire family took up residence there. Starting at five in the morning until ten at night, a veritable food factory—dispensing tiffin, coffee, meals, fruit and barley kanji—functioned next to each bed. Half-eaten idlis, bondas and chutney rotted in the nursing home's garbage bin, giving off a stench. The bin was emptied twice a day, but within half an hour of its being emptied, it overflowed again, with food from nearby hotels and the leaves they had been wrapped in. The bin was yet to be emptied that morning.

Attender Shanmugam was reading the newspaper in the reception. Though the doctor came in for consultation only at eight, three or four patients were already waiting for him.

Malati went to the dispensary next to the doctor's room and opened all the window slats. When one particular window slat was thrown open, it formed a sort of counter with a table attached, facing the patients in the reception. Malati called out to Shanmugam, who got up and came over.

'Have you issued tokens to these people?'

'The token box is in there.'

Malati fetched the token box and gave it to him. 'Have nurses changed duty?'

'Subbulakshmi amma hasn't come yet.'

'She'll be here soon. Go and bring the sweeper here immediately.'

'But she's already swept the hall and left!'

'The garbage bin hasn't been emptied. When the doctor comes in, it'll be the first thing he notices.'

'But she is at the doctor's house right now.'

'Tell her to come back here for a few minutes. She can clear the bin and go back.'

'Wait. I'll issue the tokens here before I go.'

Shanmugam distributed tokens to the waiting out-patients and left. Malati patched the connection to the switchboard. Almost immediately, it rang.

Malati put the handset to her ear. 'Good morning, 4452.'

'Is that the doctor?'

'No, this is the clerk at the nursing home. The doctor hasn't come in yet. Who is calling, please?'

'Connect me to his home then.'

'He'll be here in ten minutes.'

'I ask you to connect me, and you say, "ten minutes"? I must speak to the doctor immediately.'

'What is your name?'

'Why should I tell you? Are you going to connect me or not?'

Malati hesitated for a second. Then she connected the call to the doctor's house. Case histories of patients who had seen him the previous evening were lying in a corner. She started entering their details in the register.

Within a couple of minutes the phone rang again. It was the doctor this time.

'Yes, sir.'

'Malati, how many times do I have tell you not to connect calls to my home between seven fortyfive and eight o' clock?'

'Sorry, sir.'

'Don't you say "sorry" again to me. I don't like this.'

'Yes, sir.'

'I am five minutes late because of this call.'

'Sorry, sir.'

As soon as the doctor hung up, the phone rang again. Without the slightest pause, Malati began to recite, 'The doctor is not here now. Please call at 8.10. If you give me your name, I'll inform the doctor.'

'Sujana.'

Malati bit her lip. Sujana was an intimate friend of the doctor's. She must have heard Sujana's voice any number of times, but why hadn't she recognised it today? Perhaps the effect of Sashi's wedding!

Malati peeped into the reception with a small vestige of hope. The doctor saw out-patients every morning from eight to half past nine. Then he visited in-patients at the nursing home till about ten fifteen. He was reputed for his kairasi in treating patients. At the same time, he was also known for prescribing blood tests, X-rays and stool-and-urine tests even if a patient came to him with only a common cold—making them spend thirty or forty rupees. This reputation had also begun to spread. The daily crowd of patients was indeed beginning to thin, but one could not be sure. Suddenly, on some days, the crowd was huge. If it wasn't so today, she could ask for an hour's permission and attend Sashi's wedding.

The crowd was in fact small, but it was already past eight fifteen when the doctor entered his room. Malati had to prepare bills for two in-patients at the nursing home and arrange for a specialist doctor to come in and examine another patient in the afternoon. The nursing home's stock of oxygen cylinders would only last for two more days. There was a strike on for the past one week at the factory that provided the cylinders to their supplier. The workers were demanding a raise of hundred rupees in their pay. Malati tried to put away thoughts of Sashi's wedding from her mind.

An old woman came down the stairs. 'I want to see the doctor,' she demanded.

'He'll see you in your room in an hour,' said Malati.

The woman complained, 'There's no water supply upstairs.'

'You could use the bathroom next to the staff nurse's room.'

'I've been there already. There's no water anywhere.'

'That can't be...!'

'Am I lying, then?'

Before this could be resolved, the doctor's bell rang. Malati asked the woman to wait and hurried to the doctor's room.

There was a patient lying on the examining table and two others were standing beside him.

'Bed number 8 is vacant now, isn't it?' the doctor asked her.

'Yes,' replied Malati. Meanwhile, the patient on the examining table made a slight gesture with his hand.

One of the two men with the patient leaned closer to him. He immediately told the doctor, 'Give him some other bed, doctor.'

'That's the only bed available,' said Malati.

Ignoring her, he told the doctor, 'Appa says to avoid number eight.'

A small crease appeared on the doctor's face and then vanished. 'Two patients are to be discharged today, right?' he asked Malati.

'I am preparing their bills, sir. Both of them plan to leave only after rahukalam.'

'When does rahukalam end today?' the doctor asked Malati.

'At three in the afternoon.'

'That would be too late for this patient. Stasis has already set in. We must put him on oxygen immediately and give injections every hour.' The two men with the patient nodded their half-hearted consent.

Malati came back to her room. The old woman was still waiting there. Malati asked her, 'No water supply?'

'Well, it was you who told me to wait here.'

Malati called Shanmugam, 'It seems there's no water supply upstairs.'

'But you were informed yesterday!'

'And didn't I ask you to call the plumber and set it right?'

'The plumber said he wouldn't come here anymore.'

'How can he say he won't come? He's the one who's done the plumbing for the entire building!'

'He says one hundred and fifty rupees in his bill hasn't been settled yet.'

'But it was the doctor himself who struck it off his bill!'

Shanmugam stood silent.

'Anyway, ask him to come this once and do the work. I'll speak to the doctor.'

'You could have done that earlier, couldn't you?'

'What can I do now, Shanmugam? I asked the plumber to speak directly to the doctor. After nodding and agreeing in front of the doctor, he refuses to come here now. What can I do about it?'

Having completely lost her patience by now, the woman screamed, 'You people can quarrel some other time. If there is no water upstairs, you should at least ask someone to bring it up. You do promptly collect thirty rupees every day!'

'Please go back to your room. I'll make some arrangement within half an hour,' said Malati in an appeasing tone.

After the woman left, Malati went to the doctor's room. He was examining another patient. He asked Malati, 'Have you got Bed 8 ready?'

'I'll get that done immediately, sir. But it would be of great help if you could have a word with the engineer first.'

'Is he on the phone?'

'No, sir. There's a problem with the water supply upstairs. The plumber refuses to attend to it. If you speak to the engineer, he will instruct the plumber to come immediately.'

'Do not to bring such problems to me during consulting hours,' admonished the doctor in English.

'This is urgent, sir.'

The men who had accompanied the patient were not at all happy to be alloted Bed 8. One of the men suggested to Malati, 'You said some patient was going to be discharged. Why don't you have him transferred to this bed?'

'How can I have him transferred for just five or six hours? I'll try to give you a different room by evening.'

At quarter past nine, the doctor had finished seeing the out-patients. He began to check on the patients in the nursing home. There wouldn't be much pressure in the clinic's front office for another hour. However, during that one hour, she had to get a lot of things done—details of the day's out-patients had to be noted in the register; family accounts which were paid once a month had to be written separately; the specialist's visit to examine a patient had to be arranged for that afternoon; the bills for two patients to be discharged later that day had to be prepared and the money collected; and the plumbing upstairs had to be fixed.

Except for the last chore, Malati completed the rest within ten minutes. Half a mile away, Sashi's wedding muhurtam would be getting over within the next half hour. Even if wedding invitations had the muhurtam as lasting an hour or more, the thali was tied only in the last few minutes. If she started now, she could reach Sashi's wedding at the right time. Sashi would feel happy. It would satisfy Amma that her daughter had obeyed her word.

Malati went to the doctor's room and looked at her face in the mirror above the washbasin. Though her cheeks were slightly drawn in, her face was still beautiful.

Malati glanced around the room once and sighed. It was an airconditioned room, untouched by sunlight—there was a special odour to that room. At first, she hadn't liked the odour, but now it created a sense of longing in her. In Madras, there are airconditioners like this in many cinema halls, but there was no sense of yearning when she visited one of those. Cinema halls fail to evoke feelings of intimacy and belonging, because thousands visit them everyday. But this room was different. She saw every object in it daily. She saw them changing places, growing older. She knew all the secrets of the room's owner. They were not secrets she had probed and pried to learn. She came to know many things simply by sitting in the front office of that nursing home, working the switchboard and writing down the fees and accounts of patients who came there. This doctor who daily saw the human body in its extremely unattractive state will be caught in a big crisis very soon—Sujana. Sujana has the doctor in her grip. In this, she has the doctor's full consent. But Sujana has asked him to marry her. The doctor cannot leave his wife, and their son and daughter. Nor can he let Sujana go.

Malati looked at herself in the mirror again. She wondered whether this morning break was the only thing about her job that kept her from breaking down entirely and collapsing. Magazines publish idiotic and silly jokes about women. Which real woman do these fools look at, before they write jokes about women spending all hours of the day in front of a mirror? Do they know that many women never get the chance to look at themselves properly in a mirror? In Malati's home there is only a cracked mirror. The images it throws back are all misshapen, distorted. Are these idiots aware that many women feel annoyed at the very sight of their images in a mirror? Sujana can be fond of the mirror, but then, do all women have someone pursuing them, as Sujana has the doctor? Hundreds of thousands of women don't have anyone who would even turn around and glance at them. No one respects them even as animate life-forms with minds of their own. Such as Malati here.

Malati slammed her fist hard on the table and changed her train of thought. If she wanted to think about herself over and over again and fret, not even the whole day would be enough. She could torment herself some more, but it would yield no result.

Malati did what the doctor had failed to do—she telephoned the engineer. Upstairs, the water would now flow in a torrential flood. The flow could probably be stemmed only by the god Krishna himself.

Sujana entered. She asked Malati, 'Where is the doctor?'

'He's gone on his rounds.'

'Where, outside?'

'No. Here, in the nursing home.'

'There's no one in the room, then?' Bantering, Sujana entered the doctor's room. Immediately, there was a buzz on the intercom. Malati went into the doctor's room. Sujana was sitting near the doctor's table.

'Oh, nothing. Two days ago, I misplaced a key chain somewhere here. Did anyone find it lying around?'

'I did find one and put it away. Is that yours?'

'Thank you.'

As Malati turned to leave, Sujana spoke again, 'There was another old person here. Why is he not seen these days?'

'Who exactly do you mean?'

'Tall, swarthy, with warts on his face...'

'He left. Another clerk was appointed, and he has been on leave for the past ten days.'

'You people get provident fund, bonus benefits and everything, don't you?' Sujana was a partner in a small workshop.

Malati did not reply. Sujana stared intently at Malati. Then she picked up the brochure of a pharmaceutical company from the table and started reading it avidly.

The doctor came back from his rounds earlier than usual. 'Miss Sujana is here,' Malati told him.

'I know,' said the doctor curtly. He went to his room and emerged almost immediately with Sujana. 'I am going to attend some weddings. Don't fix any appointments before three in the afternoon,' he told her.

'Yes, sir,' said Malati.

'Anything else?' asked the doctor.

Malati said, 'If you could give me an hour off, I would like to attend a wedding and come back.'

The doctor thought for a moment. With Sujana next to him, his negative impulses were under check. 'All right. Inform Shanmugam before you leave. As for the telephone, give a direct connection to Staff Nurse Subbulakshmi's room.'

After the doctor and Sujana had left, Malati went to the doctor's room. To look at herself in the mirror, of course.

•———•

Sashi's wedding was taking place without the usual pomp. Because it was past opening time for offices, only people who were very close to the family were at the mandapam.

Sashi had seen Malati arrive from her seat on the wedding dais. It seemed as though she was asking Malati, 'Why are you so late?' Malati's mother was also present among those clusters of women. Malati was amazed at how her mother could be so garrulous all the time, without any reserve. Her eyes were so big they seemed about to pop out of their sockets, and her teeth appeared enlarged by accumulation of tartar. She had never been neatly dressed even when Malati's father was alive—

now she was much worse. However, Amma was a person without the slightest feeling of diffidence about these handicaps. Just as she lashed out and vanquished her daughter with her acid tongue, she was able to deal with and toss away anyone who confronted her. Malati wondered why she lacked her mother's egotism, which certainly did not originate from beauty, status or ability. It was enough if you had the courage to feel 'Who can dare do anything to me?' But was it really courage? Why couldn't it be stupidity, or brutishness? But stupidity is defined by results. So long as everything turned out right, you were courageous, daring and smart. When things went wrong, you were stupid. Like the doctor would discover in a few days.

Sashi's younger sister took Malati's hand and led her to the mandapam's kitchen. 'Tiffin got over half an hour ago. Let me see if there's something here at least,' she said.

'I don't want anything. I had something to eat before I came here,' said Malati.

'Why did you do that when you were coming here? If my mother hears of it, she'll scold you.'

Malati bit her tongue.

There was no tiffin in the kitchen, but several dishes which were prepared for the next session of the wedding feast were ready to be sampled. Sashi's sister had crowded her plantain leaf with food, even as Malati kept protesting that she did not want any. 'Don't eat your food in a hurry. Thali will be tied in the next half hour. Stay for lunch and then for the reception in the evening. You can go home tomorrow,' she told Malati and hurried away. When she was out of sight, Malati got up—it was not that she was not hungry, she did not feel inclined to eat.

'Endi, you said you couldn't come here?' Her mother enquired loudly and tactlessly. Malati gave her a big smile. The thirumangalyam was being taken around to the elders for their blessing. Malati wanted to pick it up for a moment to see how it felt to touch. True, she was older than Sashi by six months, but she was not of an age to bless Sashi's thali. Malati was afraid that her widowed mother might, in a fit of silliness, touch it like the rest of them. But she was disciplined about observing certain proprieties.

There was a minor commotion at the mandapam's entrance. Some important people must have arrived. Malati too looked towards the entrance eagerly. She gasped. There was the doctor, with Sujana.

•———•

'Endi, that woman who was with your doctor, is she married?' asked Amma.

Malati did not reply. She was both amused and sad. The question came from a person with a daughter of marriageable age. That she must arrange for her daughter's marriage doesn't occur to her. Nor is she distressed that her daughter remains unmarried. Instead, she eagerly gossips about someone who has nothing to do with her.

'I believe she is scheming to take over the doctor, his nursing home and every last thing he owns? Tell me, what's her caste?'

'Why are you bothered about what others are up to? I've come home after a day full of problems. Won't you let me have some peace for a little while?'

'What can I do but let you be? I've done that, and now you're stranded with no prospects at all for anything, and I am also stranded with you.'

'Don't keep jabbing and wounding me. The only thing I didn't do which you asked me to was when I refused a job in that Seth's company. I've told you why I refused to go there. It's not because some creep kept leering at me. But Appa had borrowed money from everyone in that company. Not tens or fifties—he'd taken hundreds and thousands. None of them ever asked me to return the money, but I felt ashamed, having to work with them all day with that money on my mind.'

Amma stopped her tirade. Malati felt somewhat consoled that the talk about Sujana had ended.

However, that consolation did not last long. Sujana kept surfacing, again and again, in her own thoughts. You couldn't say there was no truth in what Amma had said about Sujana. Sujana was educated, a graduate. She managed a company of her own. It wouldn't surprise anyone if the management of the nursing home was also handed over to her. If Sujana were to become not just her boss but also her employer's wife, what kind of relationship should Malati establish with her? If the boss or employer is a man, it's convenient for a woman in some ways. Men's expectations of women subordinates had certain clear limits. A woman who worked for men will be able—under their very noses—to protect the privacy of her personal life. For example, the doctor wouldn't be interested in learning about Malati's mother, nor would he understand if he were told. But it would be impossible to hide anything from Sujana. Sujana, an astute woman, could accurately guess, from a small gesture or even a sigh, the exchange that must have occurred between mother and daughter that morning or the previous night. Even now, as things stand, Sujana must already know a great deal about her.

Malati went to the kitchen, ate the two dosas which were kept for her, drank buttermilk from a small bowl and cleaned up. Amma had not cooked anything like a proper meal the whole day. Amma knew too well the value of a handful of rice. Even when Appa was alive, she had had to be watchful, as she was now, about everything she did. But when Appa was alive, she could rightfully ask for money for household expenses. Now she had two sons who lived in distant cities, and there was Malati. Her sons did not earn much. Poor Malati—after struggling to find and keep a job, she had now found steady work at the nursing home. The doctor paid her one hundred and fifty rupees promptly on the first of every month. In such hard times, when milk was three rupees a litre and tamarind seven a kilo, how casually did Amma treat this job! It was true that one hundred and fifty rupees did not make a big difference in their lives, and Amma understood that. But Malati—she must suffer abuse and take orders from everyone, and finally stretch out her palm on the first of every month to bring home regularly those one hundred and fifty rupees, which wasn't good for anything. Amma has never visited the nursing home, not even once. But it had been possible for her to infer things about Malati's work situation. Or else, why would she keep needling Malati about the fortune that the doctor pays her?

The tamboolam bag with coconut, betel leaves and areca nut, and the wedding sweets was lying on the floor. The sweets had not been put away yet. Perhaps ants had got to them by now. Everyone in Sashi's family had insisted that Malati and her mother come in the evening too. But neither Malati nor her mother chose to go. Wasn't it enough if you've had one meal at a wedding?

In five minutes, their tiny kitchen had acquired neatness and order. Even when more people had lived there, it had always been neat at bedtime. There were times when two or three people had to sleep in that kitchen, folding in their limbs. When Appa died, they had to keep a nightlong vigil over his body. At that time, fatigue beyond grief had forced them all, one after another, to take turns sleeping in that tiny kitchen.

Malati came to the hall. Amma had gone out somewhere. She may have gone to chat with the people in the rear part of the house. Isn't it Friday today? She's probably watching film songs, *Oliyum Oliyum,* on TV at a neighbour's house. This street is the kind that should have been content with radio. Just one household here could afford to acquire a television.

Crowds thronged that house at this hour on Fridays. They would promptly disperse at nine—a few minutes from now.

Malati couldn't sleep when she lay down. Nor did she feel like skimming through the magazines her mother had borrowed. In the guise of telling stories, these magazines—all of them— told lies, over and over again. Nine out of ten stories were about girls who were waiting to get married. Lies—as though every girl, in her yearning to be married, eyed strange men and went traipsing in the park, to the beach or the movies. Those sorts of lies. How many months was it since Malati last went to watch a film? If she went to the park and the beach, would she get even this beggar's pittance at the end of every month? With what enthusiasm or courage could she look into a man's eyes? If she did that once and let her mind run wild, surely terrible torments would follow.

Amma had indeed been to watch TV. She was back, asking Malati, 'Why are you sitting there alone, chin on your palm? Have you had your dinner?'

'Yes.'

'You could have locked up and come along too. The advocate's house is not so crowded these days. Three or four others have also bought televisions, so the crowd has lessened.'

'I'll come tomorrow, then.'

'Why don't you turn the bed around? If I lie down with my head in that direction, I just can't get to sleep.'

'I can't sleep no matter where I lay my head.'

'Why don't you tell your doctor? Won't he give medicines to his own employees?'

'If I am fool enough to tell him that I can't sleep at night, he will throw me out of the job.'

Amma did not seem keen on arguing at that hour. But on the thinnai, in the front part, the rear, in the neighbouring house —residents were arguing furiously among themselves. This raucous chatter, combined with all the sounds of the city, blew over them like a giant snake-charmer's horn. Amma turned the bed around herself and lay down, asking Malati to put out the light.

Malati put out the light, opened the window slats and checked if the door was latched. She then lay down on her bed.

'Endi, what caste is that Sujana?' asked Amma.

Malati rose immediately and turned on the light, and sat near the open window, staring out.

'I have my reasons for asking,' Malati's mother spoke again.

'Why should you know what her caste is? Of what use can that be to you?'

'One of your father's aunts lived in Malaysia, or was it Singapore? I have a hunch that this Sujana could be her daughter.'

'But Sujana is not even thirty yet.'

'Why, it's still possible that she is that woman's daughter! My youngest uncle was born at the time of my mother's second delivery. There's an age difference of twentyfive years between my mother and her brother.'

'What do you want *me* to do? Do you want me to bring you her horoscope?'

'Don't shout at me when you are there by the window. You even have the wretched light on!'

'Amma, why don't you let me be, just for a little while? Where can I run and hide in this tiny place? I have work to do all day—dealing endlessly with niggling problems. I work till eight, and come home after answering numerous questions from a dozen women like you. And here, you too pester me with the same kind of questions. You came to the marriage, didn't you? Why couldn't you have asked her? She is a close relative of yours—a lot closer than she is to me!'

'Why do you get upset about such a small thing? I asked you because she comes to your nursing home often. The whole town is talking about how your doctor is going to marry her. But when I ask you, you shut me up.'

'I am not shutting you up, Amma. I honestly don't know.'

'What is it that you don't know—her caste, or that she is going around with your doctor?'

'What is it to you if some woman goes around with some man?'

'Oh, nothing at all. But there shouldn't be any talk tomorrow that you are going around with the doctor.'

'Amma!' said Malati, aghast.

'I am not saying anything wrong. When a man with wife and children shamelessly escorts another woman everywhere, even to weddings, wouldn't people wonder whether he misbehaves with other women who work for him?'

Paying no further attention to either Malati's insomnia or the light that was still on, Malati's mother turned over and went to sleep.

Malati had not expected such passion from the doctor's wife. This docile woman who had stayed at home with her children, cooking regular meals for her family, barged into the doctor's room one morning when the doctor was on his rounds, and sat down in his chair. Within the next two minutes, Sujana arrived, as though the event had been preordained. Before Malati could tell her that the doctor's wife was in his room, Sujana had opened the door and entered. She came out immediately. 'Why didn't you tell me there was someone in there?' She angrily asked Malati in English.

'But you never gave me a chance to tell you. You went straight in,' replied Malati.

Now the doctor's wife too had come into the reception. 'What's wrong with her?' she asked Malati.

Malati turned to Sujana.

'When I am asking you what is wrong with her, why do you turn to her without answering me?' asked the doctor's wife again in a loud voice.

Sujana told Malati, 'Tell the doctor when he returns that I had dropped in,' and turned to leave.

The doctor's wife addressed Sujana this time, 'Where are you going? If you came here to consult the doctor, stay back and see him. Or your disease will get worse.'

'You had better speak to me with respect,' said Sujana.

'You feel I don't show you enough respect? How could that be? You've wandered into this place like a stray dog, and I haven't kicked and chased you out—isn't that respect? How much more respect do you want? Should I prostrate myself at your feet? If you had a husband and children, a hundred people will pay you respect. But you are a woman who lusts after other women's husbands—'

'Malati, I'm leaving,' said Sujana, as she began to move out.

'Hey, why are you telling *her*, of all people? The rightful owner is over here. So you're leaving? Leave, then, you have my blessings. Don't come back. Are you hurt that I haven't offered you kungumam when you are leaving? Now, are you worthy of receiving manjal and kungumam from me? Doesn't seem so, looking at your face...'

'You are going to pay for this. Be careful, don't go too far with that tongue of yours!'

'Who are you to tell me that? You barge into my house and you're teaching me respect, and how to speak? This is *my* house, *my* place, and he is *my* husband! Just get out. Watch where you're going though—you may rub yourself against four more men if you don't.'

Sujana who was about to cross the doorstep stopped abruptly. 'What did you say?'

'Have you grown hard of hearing? Show yourself to a good doctor.'

Sujana marched swiftly back into the reception. She slapped the doctor's wife hard on her face. Shanmugam and Malati, who had been watching from a distance, leapt in. Malati went to Sujana, and Shanmugam placed himself between Sujana and the doctor's wife.

The doctor's wife started screaming loudly, 'Whore, low-caste bitch, mongrel dog! You are a viper that's come to destroy my family! The man who's tied my thali has never laid a finger on me, but this mincing glamour doll raises her hand and slaps me! And there is no one to speak out at this outrage! May a snake bite that woman's hand! She raises her hand and slaps me, tries to murder me in my own house, in front of my own people!'

The doctor had meanwhile heard about the uproar and had rushed back. He turned to his wife and asked her, 'Who asked you to come here?'

She glared at him angrily, her eyes blazing, 'Who are you talking to? Do I need anybody's permission to come here?'

'There are four heart patients upstairs, and you come in here and make such a racket! What will they think? Is this a nursing home or a market? Go home. I'll come and talk to you later.'

'Who is she? Why does she come here? Does she feel so privileged that she dares to hit me!'

'What's this nonsense about beating and biting? Go home, now. Malati, take her home right away. Miss Sujana, please wait for ten minutes. I'll be right back.'

Malati laid her hand on the doctor's wife's shoulder. She bristled and flung it away. 'Leave me alone! You have to struggle for the sake of two meals a day, and you're telling me what to do? Are you here to work, or to seduce him? Chee, get away from me!'

Malati's body began to tremble. The doctor's wife had screamed such vile abuse at Sujana! That had seemed like a play or a movie. When the abuse was directed at Malati, her perspective changed. Malati unconsciously moved towards Sujana.

The doctor realised that the situation was getting out of control. He grabbed his wife's hand and dragged her towards their house. She kept shouting, 'Aiyo, aiyo!' as she was being dragged. The doctor must have pushed his wife in, latched the door from outside and returned to the nursing home.

Though Sujana too had been in a rage, she had not known how to speak out and show her anger. Even though she had slapped the doctor's wife, fear of consequences, so typical of the urban middle class, must have paralysed her, thought Malati. City-bred men and women were all cowards who died many times over in their petrified imaginations. Could any of them muster the courage to act like the doctor's wife had, at least for those few minutes?

The doctor came back to the nursing home, his hair and clothes in disarray. He told Malati, 'Inform everyone that I won't be in today and tomorrow.' Then he turned to Sujana and apologised, 'I am very sorry. I didn't know that this was happening.' When Sujana did not respond, he said, 'Come, let's go.'

Then Sujana spoke, 'I want something to be resolved this very minute.'

'Not here, please,' the doctor pleaded.

'You could have anticipated this and made sure it didn't take place.'

'No, no. I didn't expect anything like this at all.'

'Didn't you? Then I am very disappointed in you.'

Sujana looked at Malati. Malati recognised a glint of hostility that hadn't been present earlier.

•———•

For the next few hours, the nursing home felt like a madhouse to Malati. Without checking whether the doctor would actually come in that day, Shanmugam had issued tokens to patients who were waiting to consult the doctor.

An in-patient who was completely cured and waiting to be discharged slipped and fell down in the bathroom, injuring his forehead. A woman suffering from acute respiratory difficulties was brought in for admission; an hour later, they rushed her to the Royapettah Hospital in a panic. The staff nurses could not cope with having to respond to endless queries. The specialists, who were due to come in that day and the next came in punctually, but were unable to learn about patients' case histories. They were surprised—how could a doctor behave so irresponsibly?

Sujana left, with the pleading doctor in tow. Immediately after they left, there was a phone call from his house. Malati went over, unlatched the door and came back. Knowing that the doctor was away, his wife intensified her tantrums and acted in even greater fury. She went to the doctor's room, opened all the drawers in his table and cupboard, and flung his papers all over the room. When her rage seemed to have subsided a little, Malati handed over a small leather briefcase to her. 'I used to keep this with me in the reception. But I don't plan to come here anymore, so I am handing this over to you. I can manage two meals a day.'

The doctor's wife looked up at Malati. 'Will you send my elder brother a telegram?'

'Where does he live?' asked Malati.

'In Guwahati.'

'Telegram saying what?'

She considered this. 'Shall we say the doctor's killed me?'

Malati said without laughing, 'Wouldn't that seem very odd? What if your brother files a report with the police?'

'Oh, let him. Let the police come here a few times. Let them question him about the way he is betraying me.'

'As far as I know, the police won't intervene in matters like these. They would say, "Keeping your husband is your concern. We won't interfere in that."'

The doctor's wife was silent for a while. Then she said, 'You are the person who has betrayed me. So much has happened, and you never told me about it.'

'Look here, mami. That's not my job, nor will I do that. I am not concerned about your personal life, or the doctor's. I've handed over the briefcase. It contains your husband's chequebook, passbook and everything else. The accounts have been updated till yesterday. Salary for twentytwo days this month is due to me. Ask him to send word to me if he wants me to come back to the job. I'll come if I can.'

Malati left the nursing home without looking back. Only after she had taken a few steps did it strike her that she had left her pen behind. Let it go. Let the evil that had trapped her be gone with that wretched pen.

'I won't ever leave you.' Amid many giant advertisement hoardings, a small wall poster bearing that threat and promise caught Malati's eye. Someone, out of his extreme desire for someone else, had left this lovelorn message on that wall—'I'll never leave you.' Message through the wall. Message by the wall. Message on the wall. Message from the wall. Blank wall, blank wall.

Now Malati has once again turned into a blank wall. Amma has been telling her for years to join that company where Appa had worked. Let me do as Amma wishes this time. She would be interested in hearing about the lovely bonus Sujana had received today from the doctor's wife. The doctor's wife says to Sujana, 'I'll never let you have him.' She says, 'I'll never leave you,' to the doctor as well. Can the doctor, too, leave his wife? He is unable to let go of Sujana, either. Can Sujana leave the doctor? It looks like she can. In this threesome, Sujana is the one whose situation is least complicated. Confronted by the doctor's wife, she couldn't retort word for word—she could only slap her. If you have an affair with a married man, this kind of situation is bound to happen someday. Women can't be trusted. That doctor's wife, who had stayed quietly at home like a timid rabbit in its burrow—she had made such a row!

Malati was hungry. People were on their way to schools, colleges and offices. After the first meal of their day, they were hurrying to begin the first part of the day's work. Buses crawled on the roads, weighted down with people on one side, spewing out smoke from another. Taxis and autorickshas were plying energetically. Even cyclericksha-drivers, as they ferried clusters of schoolchildren on their vehicles, were imbued with a special radiance. After she began working in the nursing home, Malati had been forbidden these morning scenes. Now she can see these and more, thanks to Sujana.

The doctor must now be asking Sujana's forgiveness. Then he would go to his wife and ask *her* to forgive him. Perhaps he may even come and ask *me* to forgive him. For my wife spoke slanderously of you, I apologise to you on her behalf. Please forgive and bestow your generous blessings on me. Go away, you cretin. For the one hundred and fifty rupees you give me, I have to take—apart from the abuse from my mother at home—the title of a harlot in the outside world. And in the end, I should forgive you, too? Go. Get lost. Keep chasing Sujana. Sujana for fun. And your wife for toiling at home. Your wife, with her brutishness and stupidity, will keep driving you back to Sujana again and again. If not Sujana, then someone like her. Women are women's worst enemies.

Malati vowed that she would never earn the enmity of any woman. When she realised that there was no likelihood of putting her resolution through the smallest trial, Malati felt immensely sad.

Those Two

Venkatachalam, son of Mahalingam and grandson of Subbiah of Kizhavur village, once happened to be in the temple town of Vaitheeswarankoil, when a distant uncle of his—Sabesan—took him surreptitiously to a certain house in that town.

When Venkatachalam visited that house again, he went unaccompanied, and he was sixteen. Though he was turned out on that occasion by Dhanam's mother on the euphemistic pretext that Dhanam was 'not at home'—indicating that she was having her periods—he found it impossible not to think about her constantly.

Barely an year-and-a-half had passed after his father Mahalingam's death, when Venkatachalam, who was twentytwo at that time, forced a partitioning of the family properties, bought some land and a house at a place called Saminathapuram, and settled down there with his wife Vaala, and their children. Saminathapuram happened to be the right distance from Vaitheeswarankoil—he could get there driving his own bullock-drawn carriage.

But one night, before the end of the third year of his moving to Saminathapuram, while he was taking his carriage across the river, both wheels of the carriage got stuck in the sand. In his impatience, Venkatachalam beat the bullocks savagely. One of the bullocks, when goaded in a sensitive spot, gave a fierce snort and suddenly leapt forward, leaving the other bullock behind, thus causing the carriage to overturn.

It was four o'clock, early next morning when Venkatachalam was carried back home. Though there were no outward signs of injury, there was a continuous trickle of blood from his ears and nose.

Upon hearing that the carriage of the playboy of Kizhavur had capsized and that he was grievously hurt, Dhanam started at once to see him, much against the advice of those at home. But having come upto the street corner—one wonders what made her do it—she spent half-an-hour just sitting inside her coach and returned home. Venkatachalam died that evening without regaining consciousness.

The news of this death, unlike the news of Venkatachalam's injury, did not reach Dhanam immediately. Though it was common knowledge throughout the town, four days had passed before she came to know about it. And then—if those half a dozen people at home had not held her down locking their arms round her, she would have set fire to the roof and slashed herself wildly with a chopper. That did not happen, but the hysteria of that day resulted in a miscarriage. Her body and mind never recovered from the trauma.

Relatives claiming every kind and degree of relationship, relatives who had boycotted Venkatachalam while he was alive—now turned up for his last rites. As was generally expected, Venkatachalam had not left a will. Anyway, not much remained, except the house and a coconut grove. Vaala's father screamed that the earlier partitioning of properties had not been equitably done and that he was going to sue them.

Venkatachalam's mother, who was already heartbroken because of her son's conduct, promised that she would ensure that her share of the family property and jewellery went to Vaala and her children. She also gave an assurance that she would take care of the children for six months of the year.

Venkatachalam's eldest son Visu, who was used to playing about as he pleased in the agraharam and near the public bathing tank of Saminathapuram village, suddenly found himself uprooted to live among strangers. This left him bereft of his natural laughter and confidence.

Visu was quite dark in complexion unlike Venkatachalam and Vaala. Though he was six years old, any clothing round his waist felt as heavy as steel armour to him. But there were a lot of other children in the place where he had to live after his father's death, that he had to wear at least a waist cloth. And he also had to go to school with those children.

During the year Visu spent with his father's parents, children of his age were doing addition and subtraction, while he was still behind with his alphabet. Though unsure of his letters, he was able to identify the numbers shown to him. But he was not able to repeat or write down anything in sequence. Perhaps, as far as he was concerned, it seemed absurd to look for coherence or order in this world. As a result, he was constantly ridiculed by the other children in the school and frequently thrashed by his teacher.

The atmosphere at home was the same as it was at school since all his cousins happened to be doing well at school. Though his face was devoid of cheer, Visu's body was growing at a normal pace. It had the look of highly polished ebony.

Visu was now past being considered a child and since everyone had concluded that no amount of special attention was likely to bring about any change in him, even his mother had given up keeping tabs on his whereabouts and actions. Visu too had found out that as long as he went to school on time and was present at home for the two meals, his solitude would remain unassailed.

There was a bathing place with a flight of steps on the riverbank where the entire village bathed, but Visu always went and sat at a spot half a mile away where the cart-road from the village descended into the river. Unless it was the season for floods, the water was hardly knee-deep in this part of the river. There were also a few shoals of sand in that part of the river, which looked like small islands.

One day Visu sat digging the fine sand on one of these sandbanks until small springs of water began to well up. It would become quite dark in a few minutes. At the spot where Visu had been digging the sand was black. He felt as if his whole being had been gathered up as sand in his hands. He also felt the presence of someone else.

'Appa!' Visu called.

'Yes, my darling child!' replied Venkatachalam.

'Do you know how to build a house with sand? What I build keeps collapsing.'

Together with Visu, Venkatachalam dug the sand and piled it up to look like walls. The scarlet sky was turning to ashen grey. Venkatachalam and Visu created whimsical structures of sand. They made gaps on all four sides of the walls, which were supposed to be doors. They also built a temple tower in the centre. Visu was excited and happy. From one of the springs he had dug up he scooped up some water with both hands and lashed it over the tower. With a wobble, the tower came down. Venkatachalam let out a long sigh. Visu broke into peals of laugher. It was months since he had laughed heartily.

Suddenly Visu asked, 'But Appa, you died, didn't you?'

Venkatachalam laughed, 'What do you know about death?'

'You were set fire to and burnt.'

'Do you think it was all over with that burning?'

'But you didn't come home after that.'

Venkatachalam did not reply immediately. After a pause he said, 'That's true.'

'Please come home, Appa.' Visu said, 'Even Amma hits me.'

Then, as he looked up at his father, Visu hastened to add, 'Don't cry, Appa. You needn't come if you don't want to.'

'Yes, my dear, hereafter I can't go to anybody's house.'

Visu lost interest in Venkatachalam's homecoming and concentrated on digging the sand for water. After he had dug a wide basin and the hollow was filled with rising water, he turned to look. Venkatachalam was not there.

Visu began to feel hungry. Abandoning the house he had built and the springs he had dug up, he ran towards the bank, splashing the river water as he ran. The river was rising. Just as he reached the bank, a bullock carriage came fast and descended into the water. He saw the man in the carriage and called, 'Appa!' But there was no response.

As Visu stood watching, the carriage crossed the river and could no longer be seen. With the exception of a solitary bather some distance away there was no one else in the vicinity.

In high spirits now, Visu skipped along. Darkness had descended.

•———•

One night a week later, shouts of 'Thief! Thief!' were heard from a certain house in Vaitheeswarankoil. The neighbours armed themselves with staves and crowbars and went to look. They found a boy of seven or eight, stiff because of the cold weather, lying near the well at the backyard of the house. They took him inside the house, rubbed his body all over, wrapped him in a blanket, and made him drink a dose of pepper decoction. As soon as the boy was able to open his eyes, he called out, 'Appa! Appa!'

'Who is your father?' asked an elderly woman.

'There! Appa is standing there!' said the boy looking at the door.

They knew that he must be a brahmin despite his extremely dark complexion. But two days passed before they got to know further details of who he was and where he had come from.

It was a puzzle however, as to how this dimwitted boy, who couldn't even properly say who he was, had covered nearly twentyfive miles on foot in five or six hours, crossing the river at three places—to reach this town and the backyard of this particular house. When the boy's people came to take him back, Dhanam locked Visu in her arms and wept so much that everyone present was deeply moved.

The elders in the family ensured that Visu went through the ceremony of wearing the sacred thread even before he completed seven. This was not because they were in a hurry to make him a twice-born. It was merely that wearing the thread would qualify Visu to perform all the rites on the first death anniversary of his shortlived father, and also the subsequent monthly and yearly memorial observances.

Visu lost the thread while bathing in the river, the very next day after the ceremony. In the next two months, he lost his thread half a dozen times. Samanna Vadyar, the priest who came to teach him the sandya vandanam mantras started bringing an extra thread for him, as a matter of routine.

Not a single mantra of the sandya vandanam registered in Visu's mind. Once—during that part of the worship where one has to look at the sun and meditate—the priest said, 'Look at the sun and imagine that he shines with all that effulgence in your chest.' Visu looked at the sun and then closed his eyes. Soon Samanna Vadyar was panic-stricken—Visu's body had gone completely rigid, like a piece of wood, though he kept standing. More than half an hour passed before Visu opened his eyes again.

The day after Venkatachalam's first death anniversary, Visu could not to be found anywhere. The next day, some people from Vaitheeswarankoil brought him back. He seemed to have gone to see Dhanam again. Venkatachalam's mother now began to abuse Dhanam uninhibitedly, calling her a prostitute who used magic potions to ensnare males, a courtesan who had wrecked families generation after generation. Unexpectedly, Visu intervened once, saying, 'Paati, don't talk about her like that. Appa would feel hurt.' His grandmother found herself unable to continue her tirade. It was as if she had come under a spell. Visu had never uttered so many words together before.

A few days after this incident, Visu's mother Vaala came to her parents' house for good, bringing Visu and his two-year-old sister with her. There had certainly been talk of her spending six months in the year here and six months with her mother-in-law. But her parents decided that she no longer had to stay with her mother-in-law. Since Vaala never contradicted her elders, she left with her father without a word of protest. Nor did Vaala's mother-in-law press her to stay back at Kizhavur.

Initially, Visu found the new place very uncongenial. Here too, there were quite a few children in the agraharam. They teased him constantly, calling him 'darky'. The teacher who conducted classes would pick on just one or two students whom he tormented with questions again and again. The eldest of Visu's uncles had a perpetual grudge against him. This uncle's wife, while serving the family food, would frequently forget to serve Visu his ghee or curry. But what hurt Visu more than anything was that the river was a mile away from this village. The people of the village used a very large lotus tank for bathing and drawing drinking water. A stagnant pond did not agree with Visu's idea of a water source. Visu, who was used to communing with the flowing water of a river, found the tank water lifeless.

First came the planting season. Then came heavy rains. After a month of rains, came the season of mists. Visu, who slept on the inner veranda that skirted the open courtyard in the centre of the house, would move to the edge of the veranda so that the mist would fall on him. One night, his grandfather dragged him back to the middle of the veranda. As he lay there, Visu peered through the darkness. He could see two fireflies shining steadily without twinkling, in the vicinity of the kitchen. They were not fireflies, he realised soon—they were his mother's eyes.

Vaala hadn't talked much even when Venkatachalam was alive. Now that she had taken shelter under her parents' roof after Venkatachalam's death, she spoke even less.

She never uttered any endearments even to her two-year-old child. She spent the whole day inside the kitchen. There was perhaps another reason why her children avoided her. Following her husband's death, her head was shaved and she was made to wear a widow's sari, as decreed by the customs of her caste.

At eight in the morning, Vaala's mother made everyone at home sit in a row on the inner veranda and served them each a helping from a stonepot of cold rice. Then she left to have her bath at the village tank. When Vaala came with a pinch of cow dung and a pitcherful of water to clean the floor after the family had eaten, she saw Visu there, struggling, unable to finish the portion he had been served. Visu looked at his mother for the first time in all those months. It seemed to him that nothing within his experience could fathom the depth of his mother's eyes.

'Eat,' she said.

That word, uttered by his mother, seemed to enlarge his stomach instantly. As soon as he took up the last mouthful of rice in his hand, Vaala started wiping the floor from one end of the veranda. Before she could reach the place where Visu was sitting, he folded up the plantain leaf on which he had been served his rice and took it to the backyard to dispose of it, and then wash his hands.

Visu did not go to school that day. He walked round the lotus tank once. His grandmother, aunt and a few other women were washing their clothes and chatting in the bathing ghat reserved for women. Visu sneaked back home.

Only his mother was home at that time. She was blowing air through a small brass pipe to kindle the fire in the mud stove. There was a large bronze pot of rice on the stove. The stove was belching out huge quantities of smoke.

Visu sat down on the floor, close to the kitchen wall. It was the first time he had ever sat in that room like that. Vaala turned to look at him just once. Then she began to blow at the stove again. Visu looked at the bronze pot. The layer of flour smeared on the outside of the pot to prevent the bronze from darkening had already turned black. His mother's face had also turned dark. The kitchen too looked black. But for the door that connected it with the inner veranda, the place had no other openings or windows. A small square of glass had been fixed on the tiled roof. The sunlight that descended through it looked like a leaning pillar. The dust particles floating in the room acquired luminescence within the column—wriggling, squirming, glittering.

Visu sat there for a long time. When the stove began to burn well, his mother peeled the sheaths of a plantain flower and began to pluck out the unusable pistils from each of the numerous flowerets. She was so absorbed in her work that it seemed as though it had been destined that she should not turn her attention to anything other than kitchen work. Even the sight of Visu sitting there—his body rigid—staring at the column of light that reached the floor from the roof, did not attract her attention. Even when her brother's wife who came in with a pot of water after her bath, looked at Visu and said, 'Ah! so when there's nobody at home, you stuff your son with jaggery and ghee, do you?' Vaala did not reply. Nor did she utter a single word, when an hour later, all the adults of the family assembled there, greatly perturbed at finding Visu frozen in a sitting position. She did not give any indication that she was troubled by her son's condition.

Visu's grandmother was certain that this was the work of some evil spirit. However, Visu's grandfather was doubtful. Generally, such things happened only to women in the countryside. A vow was made to make offerings to the temple of Aiyanar in Sattanur.

It was from the day when he was branded—ghost-stricken boy, mentally unbalanced child, murder-haunted soul—that Visu's face brightened and he began to grow tall. Even his dark complexion seemed to brighten somewhat. He had learnt to read words letter by letter. As for numbers, he could count up to fifty. But he never learnt more than half the sandya vandanam, though the priest had come home and taught him for months. One reason was that halfway through the worship, he would stiffen and stand like a block of wood. Finally, his grandmother said that he need not do his sandya vandanam any more.

When the death of Venkatachalam had already become a myth of bygone days and everyone had got accustomed to the fact that the eldest daughter of the family had been widowed at twentytwo and was fettered in the house, when all these facts had been assimilated into the pattern of daily routine—one day, Visu was not to be found anywhere. He had not gone missing after he came to his mother's parental home. Which was why nobody now thought of Dhanam or Vaitheeswaran- koil. Moreover, from this village, even Sirkazhi was eighteen miles away.

For three days the whole village searched for Visu. On the fourth day a man from Kizhavur brought the boy back. Visu had somehow managed to reach Dhanam's place, though no one could find out who showed him the way or how he went. Dhanam's mother seemed to have then sent the boy to Venkatachalam's family at Kizhavur. It had taken them two days to send him to Vaala's parents' place from Kizhavur.

Visu's eldest uncle gave him a savage thrashing with a margosa branch. His body was covered with welts, and he writhed and cried in excruciating pain. Not even then did his mother come out of the kitchen. It was his grandmother who stopped her son, saying, 'Oh! the poor fatherless child!' For four days after the beating Visu had high fever. He was made to lie down inside a room instead of the exposed veranda.

In the front portion of the house, adjacent to the room for storing grains, was the 'camera room'. This room had a door and a window. It was perhaps the darkness in this room that had earned it the name 'camera room'. It was considered the safest part of the house—utensils, jewellery, silver vessels and other such items were kept there. The key to this room was either with Visu's grandfather or his eldest uncle. They were the only people who occasionally opened the room and discussed their financial transactions there.

Visu disappeared yet again. This time Visu's uncle went straight to Dhanam's place and made enquiries. But Visu was not there. Everyone in Dhanam's house now became involved in the search. He was considered a rare treasure by them. Next, Visu's grandfather went to Kizhavur. Visu was not there either. Now their household joined the search for Visu. One full day had passed since Visu disappeared. They could find no clues.

Vaala did not utter a word even then. There seemed to be no room for any further worry or grief in that permanently sorrowful visage. It was Visu's grandmother who said, 'Visu was in the veranda that day when the two of you were talking in the camera room. So please open that room and take a look.'

At eight o'clock that night, they opened the camera room. The light of the hurricane lantern did not reveal anything new in the room at first. But when the lantern was taken closer to the wall, they saw Visu curled up in a corner, his body stiff and wooden.

But he got up by himself the next morning as though nothing had happened. He betrayed no trace of having lain in the dark room for nearly two days without food or water. No tiredness. No fear.

Everyone was getting used to Visu's oddness. Boys of his age in the village were gradually taking on more responsibilities. They had to accompany their elders to the fields and supervise the work going on there. Or go to the plantain groves and tear up those large leaves so that they would not be stolen. They stripped the husks off the coconuts. Plaited coconut fronds for roofing. Cut up and stitched the bark of the plantain to make leaf-plates, which could be used at home for eating. They tended the vegetable beds in the backyards of their homes. Plucked and threw away worm-infested leaves from the plants. Cleaned the water troughs in the cattle sheds. Climbed the roofs to realign the tiles. Wiped the hurricane lanterns clean every day, mended the wick and polished the glass with the finest ash. On market days, they shopped for things needed for the household. Got the sickle and axe sharpened at the whetstone. Kept count when paddy was milled and stuffed into sacks. They stood by their elders and helped them in a hundred jobs, small and big. Visu was of no use. Once he was accepted as something of an oddity, even his eldest uncle did not harass him. 'Let the idiot hang himself for all I care,' he would say. The only thing that Visu was ever asked to do by anybody was, 'Look after your sister for a while.'

Visu's sister Kamakshi, though three years old, could not stand up yet. At one stage she had been like any other child, turning over on to her belly, etc. Even Venkatachalam seemed to love her more than he did his son. He would carry her about quite often. In fact, even on the last day of his life he had lifted her up, played with her and carried her along when he went to harness the bullocks to his carriage. He had been wearing a freshly laundered veshti specially for his visit to Dhanam. The child had wetted it, but he had not been bothered by it. Later, someone had remarked that Yama, the god of death, had lain in wait on Venkatachalam's way because he had set out in a wet veshti.

A three-year-old baby that would lie just as it was left, exactly where it was left, was not considered a problem by anyone. No one seemed to be disturbed as to why the child had not started crawling or begun trying to stand up holding on to the wall. Vaala confined herself to the kitchen as if she felt that the children were not hers at all. Initially, Venkatachalam's mother had shown some interest in the child. Vaala's mother did so too, for some time after Vaala came to live with her. But in course of time it became quite normal for Kamakshi to lie soaking in her urine and feces.

After another episode of disappearing from home and reappearing after a couple of days, Visu came and sat down near his sister—something he had never done before. In the next few days he went and sat beside her again and again. Though Vaala's mother and Vaala's brother's wife were irritated by this at first, they were quick to realise that it had its advantages. Minding his sister became Visu's responsibility.

Except for the fact that he sat beside his sister, there were no other signs to indicate that Visu was interested in taking care of her. The baby continued to lie in its excreta as usual and Visu did not seem to even acknowledge it.

One day the child had been lying like that for so long and in such a state, that Vaala and only Vaala was expected to wipe it and change its clothes. Visu noticed that a teardrop rolled down Vaala's check as she wiped the body and limbs of the child and laid her down again on a fresh dry piece of cloth. Vaala herself glanced at Visu for just a moment through the curtain of tears.

As soon as his mother left the place, Visu stroked the child's head. The child didn't even know how to laugh. Visu passed his hand over the child's arms, and then caressed her legs. She lay just as before. Visu looked intently at his sister's face. Then, holding a foot of hers in his hand, he closed his eyes.

Only when he opened his eyes again did he realise that he had been reclining on the floor for a long time. He had fallen down, still holding the baby's foot. This continuous pull had distressed the baby and she had screamed. No one paid any attention to her cries at first, but when it had continued for long, everyone at home had gathered around. They were not able to pry open Visu's hand and release the baby's foot. Several hours had passed before Visu opened his eyes of his own accord.

This time Vaala's mother had panicked. She had tried to wake him by pinching and hitting his hand. When Visu woke up by himself and loosened his grip she picked up the child, who kept sobbing.

Visu went and stood in a corner of the veranda as though he was scared. The excitement began to subside. As she laid the child down on the floor, Vaala's mother suddenly looked closely at the child. She looked closely at her legs, and tried bending and stretching both legs. The child kicked both her legs. And kicked again. Vaala's mother made the child stand on her legs, while still holding her. Till that day those legs used to bend immediately. But that day, for an instant, they stood firm, supporting the body.

Day by day, Kamakshi's legs grew stronger. Within a week she began to crawl on all fours. Three or four days later she began to sit up. Before the end of the month she began to stand up by herself holding on to the wall.

Kamakshi's attempts to walk instilled new cheer into the household. Even Vaala's elder brother's wife appeared to be happy.

Vaala's father opened the camera room and took out a pair of old but heavy silver anklets. Vaala's mother, her face beaming, put them around her granddaughter's ankles. Kamakshi began to toddle. 'Thatha', 'Athai', 'Mama'—the words came one by one and she began to speak. The child began to laugh.

One day, after bathing in the village tank, Visu plucked a lotus and brought it home. His grandmother was combing and plaiting Kamakshi's hair. Visu handed the lotus to his sister. She extended her hand and took it.

'Why don't you go to school Visu?' asked his grandmother.

'I'll go, Paati,' said Visu softly.

'Don't wear this veshti, change it before you go. Go soon, Your uncles left quite a while ago.'

Visu removed his wet veshti.

'Can't you wear a loincloth underneath, you silly boy?'

There was a clothesline in the central courtyard on which hung a loincloth and a veshti, towards the end of the line. Without making any attempt to cover himself, Visu tied his loincloth. Paati turned Kamakshi's face the other way.

Visu also tied a veshti round his waist. A tablet of sandal paste and a container of sacred ash were kept in a niche on the wall. Visu took the sandal paste, wetted it with a little water and daubed it on his forehead. While doing so he looked towards the kitchen. Vaala was standing there watching her mother combing Kamakshi's hair. For just a moment. Then she withdrew into the kitchen.

Visu set off, slate and pencil in hand. His school was in the next street. But Visu went past it and walked along the cart track. The whole area had been harvested. At a distance, in a single plot of ground, a green carpet had sprung where seeds had been sown for transplantation. There were no people in any of the irrigation wells as far as one could see. The sun was getting hotter. There were no birds in the sky. Only a small lonely cloud was floating faraway. The coconut trees—planted on one side of that field of seedlings—were swaying slightly.

The cart track led up to the threshing ground and stopped there. Visu skirted the threshing ground and walked along a well-worn path which led up to an irrigation canal and ran along its bank.

The canal was dry. Visu climbed down into its bed and walked along till he reached the shade of a tree on its bank. The sand was wet at that spot. Visu sat and began to dig. Once he had dug elbow-deep, a little water began to seep in. Visu dug faster. Holding the wet sand in his hand, he called, 'Appa! Appa!' Digging a little more, he shouted, 'Appa! Appa!' He dug deeper and deeper now, throwing out the sand, calling out all the time, 'Appa! Appa!'

Suddenly, a voice responded, 'Yes, my darling?'

•———•

As the bullock carriage went through the agraharam passing house after house, the bells round the animals' necks jingling, the occupants of all the houses came out and stood. No one in the village had seen this carriage before. It went hesitantly past all the houses. After reaching the end of the street it stopped. The driver of the carriage got down. His arms folded in politeness, he made some inquiries of the elderly man who was standing in front of the last house. Then he took hold of the reins of the bullocks and slowly turned the carriage around and brought it to a house in the middle of the right side of the street. A woman, whose self-effacing presence inside the carriage had gone unnoticed, now alighted.

Visu's uncle's wife was standing in front of the house. Approaching her, the woman enquired in a low voice, 'Is this Venkatachalam Iyer's house?'

'Venkatachalam? Who is Venkatachalam?'

The woman became confused and turned to look at the driver. The driver looked blank.

The woman looked as if she was about to collapse in disappointment. Vaala's mother came out the house and asked her daughter-in-law, 'What's it?'

'They are looking for the house of some Venkatachalam.'

Vaala's mother was taken aback for a moment. 'Why? What for?'

The woman immediately came to Vaala's mother and fell at her feet in obeisance.

'Who are you? What brings you here?'

The woman gave a reply steeped in years and years of sorrow, 'I am Dhanam.'

Vaala's mother transformed—as if she had become the fearsome Kali. 'You sinner! Can you ever hope to be happy? You who made my daughter a widow! She's had her head shaven and now crouches in a corner. How can you ever prosper? You ensnared that good man and milked away his wealth and then snatched away his life. May ruin befall you! May your body be infested with worms! May you rot inch by inch. May you stink! May you have nobody to call yours—nobody even to put those last few grains of rice in your mouth after your death. How dare you step on my threshold after being the ruination of my son-in-law. What made you come here? Having bewitched the father, are you trying to do that to the son as well?'

A crowd had collected in the street. Dhanam stood listening to everything, her head bent. Her driver stood aghast, close to the carriage. Though Vaala's brother and father were not there, some village elders had reached the place by now. On seeing them, Vaala's mother controlled herself.

'What's all this quarrel about? And who are you?' asked one of them, addressing Dhanam.

Dhanam said nothing in reply.

Another man whispered into the first man's ear.

'So you are Damayanti's daughter, are you?'

Dhanam stood silent.

'Look. If there's any money due to you, go and ask the people in Kizhavur. Or else file a case and fight it out. Why have you come here? This is a heartbroken family. If they had known that Venkita was this sort of a man, they would never have given their daughter in marriage.'

While the elderly man was talking, Visu came in from somewhere. As soon as Dhanam's eyes fell on him—her face, which had been like a wilted flower, bloomed. Forgetting her surroundings, she extended her hands and cried out 'Visu!'

Visu ran to Dhanam and hugged her. Nothing else in the world existed for Dhanam at that moment.

'Why didn't you come to see me for so long, my dear?' she said, as tears coursed down her cheeks. She pressed Visu's face close to hers with her emaciated hand.

At first no one thought of preventing this. It was as natural as a calf reaching out for its mother. Even Vaala's mother seemed to be moved for just a second. But it was she who reacted first, dragging Visu away from Dhanam. With a determination no one had sensed in him till that day, Visu pushed her hand away forcefully. Everyone stood still.

Suddenly, Visu released himself and ran inside the house. Holding his mother's hand, he brought her to the street. The men of the village had a glimpse of Vaala—in the open—for the first time in months. In fact, it was difficult to say which was Dhanam and which was Vaala.

Dhanam looked at Vaala. And Vaala did something she had not done for long—she looked at Dhanam straight in the face.

Her lips trembled in an attempt to say something. A steady stream of tears flowed from her eyes too. Dhanam called out in a weak voice, 'Akka!' Vaala enfolded Dhanam in her arms. And Dhanam too embraced her.

News must have reached Vaala's father by now. He rushed like a madman towards the two grieving women. 'Di, Vaala! You wretch! What's all this? Go inside. Go in, I say.'

Vaala looked at her father. The part of her widow's sari that was draped round her shaven head had slipped down. She pulled it up again. She looked at Dhanam's face once again. Then—her whole body shrinking—she walked away towards the well.

Dhanam was not able to hold Visu in her arms again. Visu appeared thoughtful for a moment. Then he ran into the house once again. When he came out, he was carrying his sister Kamakshi.

Visu held out Kamakshi to Dhanam. She gathered up the child eagerly and rained kisses on her face. Then putting the child down, she groped about her own waist and brought out a coin that she had kept tucked there, and placed it in Kamakshi's hand. It was a gold sovereign with King Edward's face embossed on it.

Slowly, Dhanam turned towards her carriage. The crowd parted to give way. Visu accompanied Dhanam. Before climbing into the coach Dhanam hugged Visu once again. Then she got into the carriage and sat down, huddling into a small bundle. The carriage began to move.

An hour had passed since Dhanam's departure, when Vaala's brother who had gone out returned. The whole agraharam was still agog with excitement and had not yet recovered from the day's happenings. The moment he set foot in the village, news reached him that the concubine of his sister's husband had paid them a visit. A little farther, he also learnt that this woman and Vaala had wept hugging each other. He entered the house in a rage bellowing her name.

His mother felt that the day must have dawned at an ominous hour. It was she who responded, 'What's the matter?' Ignoring her, he went to the kitchen. Vaala was not there. He went towards the well. Vaala was there huddled in a corner of the backyard. Noting the speed with which her brother was approaching, she crouched even closer to the well.

He went up to her and slapped her on the cheek. It seemed as if she had shrunk not because of the beating, but for some other reason. He, however, was impervious to all that and went on hitting her on the face and shoulders. Vaala kept moaning 'Anna! Anna!'

'You won't keep to a corner in the house, but would go to the street! You bitch! As a woman who has lost her husband, your fate is to be cooped up at home. But you want to go gallivanting, do you? You ill-fated bitch, your ill luck has consumed your husband, and now you come here and dance, do you?'

His mother came running, as he grabbed Vaala by hand and pushed her towards the manure pit. She cried out, 'Don't touch her, she is having her periods.'

Vaala sat by the manure pit, cringing. He stood there, prohibited from touching her and also disgusted with himself, 'Why didn't you tell me that before, Amma?'

'You didn't gave me a chance to say anything.'

'But weren't you shamed to see what happened here?'

'What could I have done? How can I prevent it if some woman from somewhere makes her appearance here?'

'But *this* wretched woman—you could have restrained her.'

'Poor thing! It's not her fault.'

'If a prostitute knocks on our door, does Vaala have to receive her?'

Vaala's mother desisted from mentioning Visu's name. But as her daughter-in-law made her appearance, Vaala's mother lost hope of protecting Visu for much longer. She addressed her daughter-in-law, 'Echumi, pour some water on your husband's head to wash away that polluting touch.'

The manure pit was directly behind the well. Vaala's brother gave her a nasty look. Vaala got up and walked away to another part of the backyard. Her brother sat down, and his wife drew water from the well and poured it over him. She said, 'You've just returned home and here you are made to bathe, as though you've come back from a house of death.'

She continued a conspiratorial air, 'The visitor didn't really come to meet this woman, but to see that boy.'

'Which boy? That ghost-ridden thing?'

'Yes. That woman embraces this big boy without trace of embarrassment in front of all these people and this boy hugs her ever so amorously. Given some more time, it appeared as if they would have bedded there.'

'Didn't anyone object to all this revelry? Wasn't my father here?'

'By the time he came, the billing and cooing was all over. Your sister came inside the house only after he came.'

He rinsed his towel. Then wearing it round his waist, he removed his veshti, and wrung it dry of water.

'And the woman gave a gold coin to that lame-legged Kamakshi.'

'Did someone bring it in for safekeeping?'

'Amma has kept it in.'

'That woman must have come here to give one gold coin and extort much more.'

'Who knows? But it is this boy who keeps hovering about her.'

'I'll break his leg.'

'Now don't do anything of that sort. Your own sister will then say you are torturing a fatherless child.'

Anyway, he was not able to do anything to Visu. For Vaala had high fever even while she was having her periods. All the same, she had to take the purificatory bath to wash away the pollution of menses. Her father and mother were filled with panic. Someone said that Dhanam must have caused some evil potion to be mixed in her food. Someone else said that the gold piece given by Dhanam was no ordinary coin, but one with an evil spell cast on it. Besides being treated by a doctor, Vaala was also shown to a priest who uttered mantras for effecting a cure. Except for the fever, Vaala had no other visible symptoms on her face or body. It was the custom in that part of the country to make a vow of an offering to the temple of Vaitheeswarankoil in cases of serious illness. But it was not done in this case. For, Dhanam too happened to be a resident of Vaitheeswarankoil, besides Lord Vaidyanathar.

•———•

Kamakshi's progress was remarkably fast. The way she talked and played, it was impossible for anyone to imagine that she used to lie there like a log till she was three years old. Even Vaala's sister-in-law found it impossible to harbour any malice towards the child.

Vaala's fever rose higher each day. Even when she lay unconscious with fever, only an occasional groan escaped her—not a single word. She drank the rice gruel that her mother gave her and lay in a corner of the inner veranda. Her younger brothers, Visu and Kamakshi were not allowed to go anywhere near her for fear that she might have smallpox. She did not ask to see her children either.

One evening, after four weeks of fever, Vaala opened her eyes and looked. The house seemed empty. Her mother and sister-in-law had gone to a relative's house to help with marriage preparations. They had taken Kamakshi along. There was no sign of her brothers. Only Visu came in, after roaming about somewhere.

Vaala looked at Visu. Visu sat down by her and stroked her face. The tears that sprang up in her eyes provided the only trace of moisture in that otherwise dry, desiccated face. Visu wiped his mother's eyes. The two of them went on looking at each other. Visu stroked his mother's arms. Then he moved down a little and stroked her feet. Holding the big toe of his mother's foot, he closed his eyes. But he was not able to keep his eyes closed for long. He moved back and sat down by her side again. Vaala looked pleadingly at him. Visu took his face close to hers. With tremendous effort, she managed to caress his face with her hands. Visu asked her, 'Amma, do you want to see father?'

She made an attempt to smile. Visu said again, 'Amma, I am going to call father.' He held the palm of her hand. All of a sudden, Vaala's face registered surprise.

It was Vaala's mother who came in first. The rest of them came in one after the other. Visu's youngest uncle lit the lantern. Vaala's mother came, lantern in hand, to look at her. The light fell on Vaala's face. After asking her, 'Will you have some kanji?' she looked intently at Vaala. Then, putting the lantern down near Vaala's head, she bent down to look. 'Why! Your face has cleared up so well! How do you feel now, my dear?' Vaala kept looking at her without answering. She touched Vaala's neck, 'The fever has come down quite a bit. Let me make kanji for you. It will give you some strength.' Leaving the lantern by Vaala's head, she went to the kitchen.

Vaala's elder brother who came in from outside went straight to the well and washed his feet. Visu was there, staring at a plantain tree. Vaala's brother too looked at it. Even in the twilight, he could see that the tree had pushed out a flowering tip.

'Come in, boy,' said Vaala's brother. 'Don't stand alone in the backyard at twilight hour.' He then went in, smeared some sacred ash on his forehead and sat down in the central courtyard to do the sandya vandanam ritual.

Vaala's mother made some kanji and took it to Vaala. Lifting up Vaala's head a little, she poured the kanji into her mouth, a little at a time. When she had given her half a tumbler of kanji, Visu came in. Vaala's mother told him, 'Your mother is almost cured now, Visu.' Visu stood without saying anything in reply. Vaala's eyes looked at Visu. Since Visu's face was in the shadow cast by the lantern, it looked as if he was narrowing his eyes to look at her. Suddenly Visu snatched the tumbler of kanji from his grandmother's hand. Sitting down beside his mother, he poured the kanji into her mouth. Vaala drank it up at once. Visu poured a second time. She swallowed that as well. Visu poured for the third time the little that was left in the tumbler. The kanji remained there, undrunk. Visu loosened Vaala's head from her mother's grip and placed it down. Immediately, he left the house.

Vaala's mother sat there for some time. Half an hour passed before she realised that she was sitting beside a lifeless body.

On the day after Vaala's cremation, the men sprinkled milk at the cremation ground and performed the sarsayanam rites. After coming back home, they put a stone down in the ground near the well and planted another stone in a corner of the veranda where a little sand was spread. A spathe of the coconut palm and a tender coconut were kept there and the rituals for the next ten days were initiated. It was noon when they sat down for their food. The new sacred thread that Visu was made to wear for the occasion was luminous on his dark torso. The aura of death had fully descended on the house.

•———•

Venkatachalam's mother and younger brother had been present earlier, even during the cremation. 'My son died and I accepted it. Now the woman he married has also left us,' said Venkatachalam's mother, sobbing. Quite a few people from Saminathapuram had also turned up. The large number of relatives assembled there made one wonder if a widow not yet twentytwo could engender such grief in the small world she knew. Farm labourers from all three villages had come, bringing their wives with them, for a last glimpse of the departed one. The vigil had lasted the whole night and then there had been the wait to let the inauspicious period of gulikai pass. When the body was taken for cremation the sun was quite hot.

The sarsayanam rites, belonged to the second day after cremation, but counted as the third day after death. Only those half-a-dozen men who had gone to cremate the body went to the cremation ground again for the ceremonies. The rest had left as soon as the body was taken away for cremation.

The news of Vaala's brother hitting her during her periods had spread. He was perturbed greatly by her death. 'That's the man who beat a woman of his family to death,' said a few even within his hearing. Though a lot of people hugged Visu and cried, Visu himself did not cry. If at all he went near the dead body, it was only when the rituals required him to do so. Even when firewood was stacked over the body and he set fire to it, his face did not reveal any signs of distress.

On the day of cremation there had been no disturbing talk. But now that the sarsayanam rites were over and everybody had eaten, a peculiar silence pervaded the house. Whenever Venkatachalam's mother lifted her head, Vaala's mother would leave the place. Once when Venkatachalam's younger brother made an attempt to talk to Visu, Vaala's father took Visu away. Kamakshi was sent to stay with a relative who lived at the end of the street. On the day following the sarsayanam, Venkatachalam's mother and brother left for Kizhavur, having said nothing. They did not take leave of anyone, as custom forbids it after a visit to a house of death.

That evening a carriage came and waited for a long time at the street corner. Visu was returning from the river when he heard his name being called softly. He went up to the carriage. Dhanam sobbed, hugging Visu. Then she climbed back into the carriage and left, no one having observed her.

On the tenth day, there was another gathering of kith and kin. The stones that were put in the ground earlier were now dug up. A mat was torn up. The women of the house had been herded into a carriage and were about to set off to the river, when two carriages brought people from Kizhavur. There was a lawyer among them. The newcomers also took part in the ceremonies.

Everyone was treated to a formal feast that day, the food being served on plantain leaves which had their tips intact. It was then that the talks began gradually. Venkatachalam's uncle—an old man—spoke first. Visu and Kamakshi cannot be left with Vaala's parents any longer. Once the functions of these thirteen days were over, the children must be brought up in the house where they belonged. It was with the intention of taking the children back to Kizhavur that the family had come.

Vaala's father did not reply. It was he who had created a scene after Venkatachalam's death, levelling charges about the way the property had been divided. The memory of that occasion perhaps lingered in the minds of all those present.

The people from Kizhavur waited for a reply. After a while, Vaala's father said, 'What is the hurry to decide that now?'

The old man of Kizhavur spoke in a conciliatory tone, 'There's no hurry. Let all the functions get over.'

'There are three more days to go.'

'Of course. After three days we'll take both the children with us.'

'But you never came to take them all these days.'

'All these days, you never allowed that to happen. It was you who brought Vaala and the children with you. You refused to send them back to Kizhavur.'

'Please tell them that the children are attached to us,' called Vaala's mother, speaking from the kitchen.

'It is not as though they do not like us. With children, it is only a matter of getting used to certain people.'

'How could they get used to you, when you made our daughter a widow and cast her away?'

For a moment, there was silence. Then the old man spoke, 'Do not speak in haste. Rightfully, even the ceremonies of the past ten days ought to have been performed in our house. We ignored the convention only because we did not want to aggravate your grief.'

Vaala's mother wailed, 'My womb that gave birth to her is now all afire!'

'It is my womb that gave birth to him that is on fire!' screamed Venkatachalam's mother.

'Hush!' the old man stood up. 'We didn't come here to pick a quarrel. Be quiet!' he said, rebuking his younger brother's wife.

But he was not able to control Vaala's mother. She continued to shout, 'It was you who came here asking for the hand of my daughter for that womanising son of yours. You hood-winked and ruined us. You made us give our pet parrot as prey for your cat. How can your family ever flourish? Aiyo... Aiyo...'

Venkatachalam's mother could not contain herself any longer. She too began to shout, 'You evil woman! You didn't let my son live even four years after marriage. You palmed off that daughter of yours on us, knowing well that she would bring ill luck to us. All because you coveted our wealth and property. So what if your daughter was widowed? Wasn't it my son who died? After snatching my son, you now want to snatch away his children too! You never gave them enough to eat, did you? You hit and tortured the children. The whole village is mocking you for the way you have looked after them. Why, even your own daughter did not die a natural death. You people beat her to death, didn't you?'

Venkatachalam's mother continued her raving. No one could stop her now. 'You are a vile wretch! You have murdered your daughter, beating her while she was having her periods. You are a family of monstrous sinners. So what if she was your daughter? She was my daughter-in-law. She was born in your house by mischance. I would have treasured her. You didn't give her a chance to live there and you dragged her here. The poor dear was always hovering around me. Having lost my son so young, I hoped to see his wife live long. You have ruined all my hopes. Oh God! Though my son had been reduced to dust, I thought his wife at least would live. Everything is gone. Oh God, where shall I go and wail for my loss!' Unable to bear her grief, Venkatachalam's mother fainted.

Venkatachalam's brother ran in panic towards her crying 'Amma, Amma!' The menfolk moved out of the house, as though they felt that no serious matter could be decided now.

In a short while Venkatachalam's mother opened her eyes. Realising her helplessness, she began to cry. 'No, Amma, Don't cry, please don't,' said Venkatachalam's brother. 'Let's go back home.'

Visu was sitting in a corner, observing everything. At one point he even seemed to laugh. The lawyer from Kizhavur said something to one of the men who had come with him. Before leaving the room, this person gestured to Visu asking him to come. But Visu didn't budge. Vaala's mother had other chores to do. 'Look at that woman putting on an act in this house of death!' she muttered, as she took the cooking utensils to wash them at the well.

The lawyer of Kizhavur was speaking to Vaala's father, 'People will tell you a lot of things concerning the children, since they are minors now. But let me explain the correct position. Even the house and land in Saminathapuram are ancestral property. There is a mortgage of eight thousand rupees on them. The documents are all in your son-in-law's name. The loan and the interest on it together have grown to more than ten thousand by now. As for the jewellery you gave your daughter, you have taken them back. A few of the silver vessels given by you are left with us. The only other things now with us are her brass utensils, trunks and bedding. Venkatachalam's mother has given quite a lot of jewels to your daughter.' The lawyer took out a piece of paper from his spectacle-case. 'Here, look at this—a heavy gold choker with a pendant of precious stones—must be nearly ten sovereigns in weight, I believe. Two pairs of gold bangles. That will come to seven sovereigns or so. A rakkodi for the head, which was made of three sovereigns of gold and gems. The making charges came to thirty rupees. They had given Visu a waist chain—a thick one with a pendant with the embossed figure of the child Krishna lying on the banyan leaf. Eight sovereigns of gold went into that. All these items were seen by our people only when they were presented. No one has seen them since. It was you who vacated the house at Saminathapuram. Only you know how much was there. When we made enquiries we came to know that your son-in-law had never squandered his wealth on that woman of Vaitheeswarankoil. In fact, it was Dhanam's people who paid for that pair of bullocks for his carriage—we have it from the man who had sold the bullocks. Your daughter is also dead now. But the children are here. It seems that Venkatachalam once expressed the wish that though he himself had not been educated, his son must study at the college in Kumbakonam. The girl has to be brought up and married into a good family. Then there's the matter of the monthly ceremonies to be performed for Vaala. Only we have the right to perform them and we are going to perform them.

'Even now we are prepared to bear the expenses of what is to be conducted here. We can perform it with the same priests you have brought in. Brahmins from elsewhere may come to receive the gifts of charity given during these functions. But our family priest shall come for the sodambam rite. We have allowed all the rituals to be done in this place. Our son was cremated outside his native village and our daughter-in-law too has been cremated in another village. But whatever the place, it is all the same earth and the same Kaveri water.'

The lawyer continued, 'I wonder if you are aware of all that's happening in your house. Rumour has it that the children are ill-treated here, and that Vaala did not die a natural death. But now that she herself is gone, whom shall we ask about what happened, and how? Each man carries his own burden of sin. We break our heads over little nothings here. But there, the Lord plays his mysterious games. Now, please inform your womenfolk as well. Let us not fight a case in the court for the children. I don't speak merely as a friend of their family, but as one who wishes you well. You can come and visit the children in Kizhavur on auspicious occasions. We shall also send them here. Think it over. In spite of our great sadness, let us celebrate the thirteenth day function of subhasweekaram as an auspicious occasion, just as the name suggests.'

The lawyer gestured with his head to someone who promptly opened a large container of betel leaves and nuts. With a nutcracker the lawyer began to slice areca nut in a deliberate and relaxed manner. He chose a good, fresh betel leaf, removed its stalk and tip, spread a little lime paste on it, folded the leaf in two along the central vein and then tore off the vein. He began to chew it. When it was well crushed, he took a pinch of tobacco with three fingers and popped it into his mouth.

Venkatachalam's brother now came out to the front. 'Periyappa, let us go back home,' he said. Before his uncle could reply, the lawyer patted him on his shoulder.

Venkatachalam's uncle went into the house. The women were now clearly divided into two groups. Somewhere in the backyard, Vaala's mother was talking non-stop to someone.

The old man went up to Visu. No one stopped him. The front half of Visu's head had been shaven closely that day. The man pushed back the stray hairs of Visu's tuft near his ear. Visu stood up.

Venkatachalam's uncle took Visu by his hand and led him to Venkatachalam's mother. Visu was silent at first. Then he addressed her softly, 'Paati!'

•———•

Trains transform according to the time of day. A train does not appear the same at night as it does during the day. For all its size, and the huffing and puffing of smoke through its head and through the interstices between the wheels, the train inspires a sense of wonder rather than fear during daytime. The people sitting inside the compartments seem diminished and look like mere dolls. At night, on the other hand, the train becomes diminished in size. One can't see it exhaling smoke. Could it be that trains do not exhale smoke at night? That's not likely either. For there are sparks that erupt suddenly, burst, burn out and vanish—all in a few seconds. The sparks signify the existence of fire. As people keep saying, there can be no smoke without a fire. Therefore smoke will certainly be found there.

Dhanam was sitting at the window of her house watching the smoke of a train that was disappearing into the distance. Early every morning, the rumbling of a train—a train that was not scheduled to halt at their town—could be heard. The headlight would flash for just a moment before it passed beyond her view. It looked like a plaything to Dhanam, not something useful. Even on those few occasions in her childhood, when she had gone on short train journeys, the train had somehow failed to inspire confidence in her. But a train was now going to take her away... far far away from Vaitheeswarankoil.

Dhanam's house was always full of people—some arriving, some leaving, and some more staying. It was not always clear who stayed there, for what purpose and with what rights.

But if there was one thread that bound them together, it was music. Great vocalists and virtuoso accompanists came there. Novices stepping on the first rungs of music lessons would also come there. Theatre folk came there too. The whole lot would be fed by Dhanam's family. The whole house and even the veranda outside would be littered with betel leaves and areca nut. In every nook and corner there would be some sleepy occupant. Dhanam's mother would wake them up for meals.

All that was going to change now. The changes had begun gradually when that playboy of Kizhavur began his liaison with Dhanam. The prosperity of the house began to decline. Spending became a strictly calculable affair. They were occasionally compelled to ask someone for money, at least on loan. The sound of music in the house, however, had not ever diminished. Nor was there any dearth of discussions on music. Musicians' visits and their demonstrations, their requests to Dhanam's mother and Dhanam to sing them—none of these lessened.

For a long time after Venkatachalam's death Dhanam did not sing. No one pressed her to sing. Then she began to sing once in a while, of her own accord. Streams of tears would flow from her eyes as she sang. Dhanam had never been called an avatar of music or a human incarnation of Saraswati. The family's least endowed in musical ability, according to general opinion, was an aunt who had joined a travelling troupe of players. Dhanam had not trained even as much as that aunt. Dhanam's only accomplishment was to sing and to be lost in her own song.

They had decided not to close their house on leaving, and to keep all the valuables locked in one room for safekeeping. With the help of hired labourers, Dhanam's mother was moving an ancient heavy iron safe to the room that was to be locked. The doorframe of the room in which the iron safe had been kept for ages, had become worm-eaten. And, it is not easy to change the doorframe in that type of house.

Dhanam had never seen the inside of that safe. It was just three or four feet in height. It had been kept mounted on a base made of thick wooden slabs. With the help of a pair of casurarina logs, it was now being pushed inch by inch towards another room along the inner veranda.

Dhanam went to the room in which the safe had originally been kept and sat down on the window ledge, in the dark. In those village houses all the rooms were very dark. But even in the darkness, the portion of the wall against which the safe had stood looked bright. A veena and two steel trunks were kept on the wooden loft of that room. Dhanam had heard that those trunks belonged to a distant aunt who had sailed away to Burma. Perhaps people had assumed that whoever left that house was bound to return some day. The trunks were awaiting the return of the aunt. No one knew for certain if that aunt was even alive.

There was some noise from the men who were moving the safe. They had positioned the wooden base in the required place and were now lifting the safe on to it. Dhanam's uncle and a boy, who was a relative of theirs, were also helping the labourers lift the iron safe. The boy had come from Cholavandan only two months ago. He had come to learn music from Dhanam's uncle. But now, in a week's time, he would have to go in search of some other teacher. Dhanam's mother had asked him to stay on in the house and had promised to arrange for tuitions with Kandasami Pillai of Sirkazhi. Kandasami Pillai was also related to the boy. He had not gone there earlier because Kandasami Pillai was reputed to hit his students mercilessly. Dhanam's uncle, on the other hand, was a very mild-mannered man. Dhanam's grandmother had an elder sister who often used to ask her, 'How is it that the people in your family have turned out to be such a bunch of harmless greenhorns?'

But Dhanam's mother never took it seriously. 'The meek can always manage to survive,' she would say. 'Those who are famed for their shrewdness are the ones who fall hard.' But now, as a result of having been timid and harmless, they had been forced to migrate from their native town.

The iron safe was finally ensconced securely. The labourers went out and stood in the hall and Dhanam's mother went in to make some buttermilk for them. Dhanam's uncle came and stood by Dhanam. He too began to look out through the window. At a distance, there was a train moving. Dhanam looked sorrowfully at her uncle. He stroked her head and moved away, without meeting her eyes.

Even Dhanam's mother had not found this decision to migrate to Madras an easy one. She had seen many people belonging to her community enjoy immense prosperity and influence and then, in their last days, lose everything to languish and die without means even for betel leaves and areca nut. An old woman once lay dead with no one claiming the body for a night and a day. The village people then had to hire men to remove the corpse. A few families that had migrated to Madurai generations ago had been driven out of the street they had been living in. A man in a white robe had sprung from somewhere and went about preaching morality from street to street, harassing people in the process. Who can say where and how this kind of moral behaviour can spread? Is there anyone who is really moral? Who knows? That white-robed man's son is probably curled up at some woman's feet.

Dhanam's mother came and asked Dhanam, 'Will you have something to eat, dear?' After the miscarriage, Dhanam's health had been ruined. Anything she ate made her stomach turn and she would vomit immediately. She had met a number of doctors, but to no avail. Quite often, she even seemed to be psychologically disturbed. It was during this period, when everyone in the house was deeply worried, that Visu was discovered early one night lying unconscious near the well. After Visu came to that house, Dhanam began to improve a little. True, she never regained her former health. But she had improved considerably compared to the time when her family had feared that she would die of grief.

Dhanam drank the buttermilk her mother gave her. They used to have two cows at home. Even after the cows had been sold, two or three padis of milk used to be purchased morning and evening. All that had now been reduced to a meagre three-fourths of a padi, bought just once a day. Still, every visitor was offered some buttermilk. Quite likely that her mother would send someone to buy more buttermilk today.

Dhanam went to the well to wash the vessel in which her mother had given her buttermilk. It was possible to wash it in the courtyard. But today a number of silk saris—saris received on numerous occasions over the years—were spread out in the courtyard for airing. Every sari was sumptuously decorated with gold zari. A red benares silk sari was interwoven with gold through its entire length. Dhanam's mother had spread the saris out cleverly. Saris that were likely to make Dhanam sad were laid out at the bottom and the rest on top.

The cowshed near the well was empty except for a corner where dried coconut fronds and firewood were stacked. Once the open fireplace used to have water boiling at all hours for people to bathe. Now, water was heated only for Dhanam. The carriage and the bullocks had been given to them by a landlord of Mayavaram. Before selling them Dhanam's mother had sent someone to the landlord to get his opinion. The man, who was immobilised by paralysis, had sent word, 'Do whatever you like.' He had also sent a gift of a measure of paddy through the messenger. It was still lying unhusked.

Take the case of Shakuntala, the heroine of Kalidasa. Her marriage takes place when she is ignorant even of the fact that a girl must leave for another home once she gets married. Only when her foster-father, the rishi Kanva, returns to their hermitage several months later and arranges to send her to her husband's place, does Shakuntala realise that she has to leave the only place she has known as home—forever. Every tree and shrub and creeper in the place increases the pain of her parting. But then, though Shakuntala had parted from things that she had held dear, she had done it only to go to her husband's place... Dhanam let her eyes wander over the well and its surroundings.

The goldsmith had gone to Thanjavur to sell some of their jewellery. Half the items had been made by him. He did not have the heart to sell them locally. Each piece was bound to have a story behind it—not necessarily a good one. Fifty miles away from this place, the stories would cease to exist. All that mattered would be the total weight in sovereigns, the weight of the gems, the wastage when the gold is melted, and the final value. 'I am prepared to give you this much, OK?' The transaction would thus conclude.

Inside the house, an old woman was cooking. She and a few others were going to stay on in the house. So the household shall continue—like the container once used to store asafoetida. The flavour would linger long after the spice was used up.

For quite sometime now, the comparison to an empty container of spice had stuck to their house. One woman of the family had joined a drama troupe. Another had trusted a man enough to follow him to a foreign land. The eldest uncle, who had seemed as solid and permanent as a mountain, had been considered the 'King of Todi'—the greatest exponent of Todi ragam in that part of the country. He used to he invited by rajas and maharajas and had brought gold and money to enrich the house; he had once made two thousand rupees just by recording four songs on gramophone records. This man had died suddenly of a heart attack while he was returning from a wedding concert. Dhanam was now like Sita in the asoka grove, whom Hanuman had failed to visit. One had to console oneself that at least the container of spice had been spared, though bereft of its contents.

Dhanam's uncle came in, obviously tired after all the running about. 'Well, how did everything go?' asked Dhanam's mother and brought him a sombu of water.

'I've informed the accountant. I've also told Ganapathi Iyer. Both of them have promised to ensure that our lessee sends us at least two hundred rupees a year. I also met the postmaster. He says the gramophone company would have received our reply. So let's leave this place, resting all our burdens on God.'

He drank the water straight from the sombu. Suddenly as if he had just remembered something, he asked her in a low voice, 'Did your daughter go to that Kizhavur house again?'

'No, after we sold the bullocks, she hasn't stirred out,' replied Dhanam's mother.

'Did you tell any of those people that we are going to leave this place for good?'

'No. I didn't breathe a word to anyone. Why do you ask me?'

He was silent for a while. Then he said, 'I too feel confused about this particular matter. I don't know if what we are doing is right or wrong.'

'What exactly are you talking about?'

'Maybe we are not quite responsible for the sin of separating the husband from his wife. But whom shall we reckon with for the sin of separating these two?'

'Who are "these two"?'

'Dhanam and that boy.'

'You mean Viswanathan?'

'Yes. That man who comes to deliver our letters on the bicycle, I heard him telling the postmaster that the boy was swimming across the river and coming this way.'

The Boatmail, that pride of the South Indian Railway, was not scheduled to stop at Vaitheeswarankoil. One had to go up to Mayavaram to catch this train to Madras. Ticket fares were higher for the Boatmail—the rate per mile was higher. But if one took the passenger train from Senkottai to Madras, one could board the train even at Vaitheeswarankoil. Three people could travel to Madras, spending less than ten rupees.

Tuesdays and Wednesdays are unlucky days for setting out on a northward journey, Siva's trident being poised for a strike from the north on those particular days. Friday is the day of discord. The first day after the new or full moon, the days of the second and third lunar asterisms, the eighth day after the new or full moon, all these days are unfit for journeys. Looking for a propitious day for their journey, Vaidyanatha Sastri had ruled out all these days and finally chosen Saturday.

'A Saturday?' asked Dhanam's mother.

'Why not, Damayanti?'

'Could you choose some other day please?'

'There is no other propitious day for a whole fortnight. Then come the days of the waning moon. Saturday is a good day. A day of stability. A day favourable for dear Dhanam.'

'I somehow feel uneasy...'

'Do you think I'll ever select a day that will bring you trouble? Begin this journey without anxiety. God will make sure that you lack nothing.'

'It is only after shifting my burdens to God that I am leaving this town forever.'

'Don't say so, my dear. You must come back famous and prosperous. Even today when I think of your eldest brother, I feel like shedding tears. He was a genius! What musical learning! What improvisations! And he had such a sweet nature. It is so unfortunate that he did not live for long. What a pity!'

Dhanam's mother placed two plantains before the priest. He took them and left.

Finally, Saturday arrived. Dhanam's mother herself did the cooking that day. She placed a large potful of cooked rice before the alcove of the household deities and prostrated herself, facing the north. Then she went to the threshold and looked reverently at the temple tower and looked at the sky. It was cloudless. No birds were to be seen because of the hot sun. She sighed and came in.

A few relatives had come home. A girl in a long skirt was playing hopscotch in the courtyard. Dhanam stood on the veranda, watching her.

The girl stopped playing briefly for Dhanam's mother to pass, and began to play again. Standing on one leg, she asked Dhanam, 'Will you join me, akka?'

For a moment, Dhanam stood still, taken aback by this unexpected invitation. Then, with a faint smile, she stepped down from veranda.

The girl had drawn small squares on the courtyard with a chalky stone. An old wooden comb served as the chip that was to be thrown. Throwing the comb into the first square, Dhanam hopped over it into the other squares one by one, and rounded back to the beginning. The second square was also played smoothly. When she tried to throw the comb into the third square, it landed on the line. The girl took up the comb.

One, Two, Three, Four. When she threw the chip for the fifth square, it fell down touching the line.

'Here, you play, akka,' she said, giving the comb back to Dhanam.

Dhanam gave it back to the girl. Without saying anything, she went to the front room and sat by the window.

The temple bell could be heard ringing for the noon puja. Dhanam's mother went up to her and said, 'Go and have your bath, will you?' After bolting the back door from the outside, Dhanam went up to the well.

The well had a lever arrangement for drawing water. A long bamboo pole had a wooden tub at one end and a beam at the other. One had to hold the bamboo, push it into the well and let the tub fill with water. Then the beam on the other end would go down by itself and automatically the tub of water would be lifted up. One should be careful that the bamboo didn't come up too fast and hit anyone.

There was a broad stone ledge from which the bamboo can be guided to rise and fall uniformly. Dhanam peeped into the well. In spite of the noon sun, the surface of the water looked black because of the shadow of the well. Her face was visible in that blackness as if reflected in a mirror. A couple of butterflies were fluttering inside the well. Deep down on the wall of the well a small plant had somehow taken root.

Not in a mood for taking a bath, Dhanam sat down on the stone used for washing clothes. That was the place where Visu had been found, lying curled up. How did that boy who could not even tell his name properly manage to walk miles and miles, and also cross the river at two or three places and reach her house?

That day, her heart had been pounding even before he was identified. She—who had been frozen for so long—began to melt, upon learning that he was Venkatachalam's son. In the *Ramayana*, Ahalya, the woman who had been turned to stone had come back to life at Rama's touch. Dhanam too had been like a stone and had been given a new lease of life because of a boy. This stone she was sitting on now must have been hit many times by the clothes that were washed on it. It was bound to remain a washing stone forever. And thousands of wet clothes would be banged against it. But Dhanam would not be one of those who did so. When would she look at this stone again?

'Dhanam! Dhanam!' someone was calling out to her from behind the backyard door. She would have liked to escape through the back entrance and go away somewhere. But where could she go? The farthest reach of an unfortunate woman is the corner of the courtyard, as they say. Was there any other option for her except to hide behind her mother?

Dhanam unbolted the door. The girl and Dhanam's uncle were standing there. He asked her, 'What are you doing?'

'I have to bathe.'

'For half an hour?'

'But I didn't bathe.'

'Don't get cross now, dear. I just asked because you've taken so long.'

'I don't want to bathe,' said Dhanam, going past them to enter the house.

Dhanam's uncle did not hear her. He too went in. Dhanam's mother asked him, 'When did you ask for the carriage to be sent? Subramanian is already here!'

'But I told him to bring it only after three. Where is he?'

Subramanian was unharnessing the bullocks. Dhanam's uncle said to Subramanian, 'So you are here. Good. Does your master know that the carriage can be returned only late in the evening?'

'Yes, sir. There's no shade for the bullocks here. Shall I take them to the backyard?'

'Yes, and leave them tied there.'

Subramanian led the two bullocks through the interior of the house. The animals stepped over the threshold carefully, climbed down into the courtyard and up again and went towards the well.

Dhanam's mother made everyone sit down and served the food herself. She divided the sweet lentil payasam among them, keeping just a small ladleful for herself. The feast was eaten in silence. The girl who had been playing hopscotch removed the plantain leaves from which they had eaten and wiped the floor clean.

After giving some food to Subramanian who had brought the carriage, Dhanam's mother had her meal. Then she took a few large utensils from the kitchen to the room with the iron safe. Except for Dhanam and her uncle, everyone else kept watching intently. When Dhanam's mother turned a pot upside down, emptied the water, and wiped the inside of the vessel with a cloth, an old woman who could not bear it any longer asked her, 'Why do you want to lock up even that thing? Aren't we supposed to live here?'

'There's another pot in there, Periyamma,' replied Dhanam's mother. After a pause, she continued, 'This is not even ours. It had been pawned by someone a long time ago. If the man comes to claim it, shouldn't we give it back?'

The old woman tut-tutted. Dhanam's mother took a few more items that were to be kept in the locked room and came back. She looked at Dhanam and said, 'Couldn't you have combed and plaited your hair after you had your food? Do I have to tell you even this?'

Dhanam moved away from there reluctantly. As soon as Dhanam was out of sight, Dhanam's mother went to her aunt. Sitting down beside her, she spoke in a low voice, 'Periyamma, it is only the presence of all of you here that gives us the courage to leave for Madras. I'll send you whatever I can from there—may be twenty or thirty rupees every fortnight or twenty days. I have been to see the postmaster and have talked to him personally. He will come here and give it to you. If you don't say a happy goodbye to us, it would really distress me.' She touched the old woman's feet in obeisance. Getting up at once, she went to the room where Dhanam was.

Subramanian had harnessed the bullocks to the carriage and made it stand facing the east, although it blocked half the street in that position. After looking at both ends of the street to make sure that the omens were good, Dhanam's mother brought the first box herself and lifted it onto the carriage. Two more boxes and a roll of bedding were then heaved up. A bundle containing their food package, a brass kooja of water and a basket were left near the front steps of the house. The front portions of every house in the street were filled with people.

Dhanam was still sitting on the inner veranda. Dhanam's mother went up to her said, 'Get up.' Dhanam stood up. She looked beautiful in a black sari, with her hair in a neat braid after a long, long time. But she had not daubed her forehead with a pottu, as though she were a widow.

Dhanam's mother checked the lock of the room with the iron safe by pulling it. Then she peeped into the kitchen, inserted her hand into something, brought the hand close to Dhanam's forehead and daubed a pottu mark on it, accomplishing the whole action with a single sweeping movement of her hand. 'Come on,' she said. Dhanam followed her.

Dhanam had to get into the carriage first. The basket was then handed over to her. Dhanam's mother climbed in next, carrying the bundle of food. She sat on the opposite side, facing Dhanam. Dhanam's uncle got in last. He was the only person in the group who possessed a pair of sandals. He tucked them on to the inner wall of the coach. The kooja of water was handed over to him.

Subramanian climbed up in front, and the carriage gave a jolt. Dhanam's mother craned her neck as far as she could to see who were passing by on the street. She looked at her relatives standing in front of her house. 'Let me take leave then. Take good care of the house. Periyamma, goodbye.' She watched the street as she said this.

Dhanam's uncle said to her mother, 'Let's start. The whole street has gathered here to watch the fun.' But Dhanam's mother still kept watching the street. There were no passers-by at that time of day.

Subramanian turned to look inside the carriage.

Dhanam's mother said, hesitantly, 'All right. Start.' The coach moved and turned as though it too were starting half-heartedly.

Upon reaching the end of the street, they had to take a left turn to go to the station. The coach turned. Suddenly Dhanam cried, 'Stop! Stop!'

No special effort was needed for Subramanian to stop the carriage. Pushing her mother aside, Dhanam came to where her uncle was sitting. Then pushing him aside, she tried to lift the iron rod barring the entrance of the carriage. The rod was inserted into a ring of metal and was held tightly. Impelled by the force with which Dhanam was pushing him, her uncle eased the rod up involuntarily. Dhanam jumped down from the carriage and began to run in the opposite direction.

'Catch her, annachi!' shouted Dhanam's mother to her brother. He too jumped down from the carriage. The kooja and the basket fell down from the carriage due to the impact and rolled on the ground. Subramanian leapt down too.

Dhanam ran. She was followed at a brisk pace by her uncle and behind him, her mother. It was a cart track with trees and bushes growing thick on either side. Despite the need to stop Dhanam which was urging him on, he could not help realising that his feet were hurting for he had left his sandals behind in the carriage. But Dhanam was running as though her feet did not touch the ground at all. Only when they reached the open ground, leaving the trees and bushes behind did the reason for her running become evident.

A dark figure could be seen at a distance, walking towards them. As soon as it caught sight of Dhanam, the figure began to walk faster. Soon it began to run.

Dhanam in her black sari and Visu who wore just a white veshti his waist fell into each other's arms. When Dhanam's uncle and a little later, her mother reached them, Dhanam was sobbing her heart out, hugging Visu.

Dhanam's uncle separated her from Visu with great tenderness. He looked intently at Visu. Visu too met his eyes without the least hesitation.

Dhanam's mother spoke to Visu, 'Goodbye, my dear boy. You must stay at your home now. Why did you leave your little sister behind and come here? Who will look after her? Go back, child. Dhanam is going to Madras. If you come to Madras when you are quite grown up, you can visit us there. If we happen to come here, I'll send word to you. Now go back. Dhanam will come with us only if you say goodbye to her. Say goodbye.'

Visu looked at Dhanam. 'Goodbye, Amma,' he said.

Dhanam embraced him again.

Visu again said, 'Goodbye, Amma. I came here just to say goodbye.'

Dhanam's mother nudged her. Dhanam spoke for the first time, 'Visu, will you come to see me before I die?'

'Yes, Amma, I will.'

'But they are taking me far, far away, Visu.'

'No matter how far it is, I will come.'

'Visu!'

'Amma!'

'Wherever I may happen to be, you will come to see me, won't you?'

'I will, Amma.'

'Even if you don't get to see me, you will come to light my pyre, won't you?'

'I will come, Amma.'

Dhanam's mother dragged Dhanam away, pulling her hand. Dhanam looked once at Visu and went along with her mother. After going some ten feet, she turned back to look.

'I will come, Amma!' Visu said loudly. Without waiting for a reply from anyone, he turned and walked away.

When Subramanian brought the carriage to the station and stopped, another mother and daughter pair were the only people waiting for the train. A baby that must have had its head tonsured that day was lying asleep on the daughter's shoulder.

The stationmaster of Vaitheeswarankoil rang the bell by hitting a hanging piece of rail with a small piece of iron, and then put on a white shirt which hung loose on him. Then he called those who were sitting on the station platform and issued them tickets—two for Chidambaram and three for Egmore, Madras. Dhanam's younger uncle and the boy from Cholavandan were at the station, having come on foot. The bullock carriage had been necessary because of the women and the luggage.

Though the platform was half a furlong in length, the station itself was just big enough to be called a hut. Only the edge of the platform was paved with stones. The rest of it was just earth. Inside the hut-like room, a man in a blue shirt was cleaning the railway lanterns and filling them with oil.

Seated on top of a steel trunk, Dhanam was watching the horizon. Sitting outdoors in the evening soothed her heart. It was very different from watching the sky sitting inside the house. Some distance away on the eastern floor of the platform, were Dhanam's mother, her younger brother and the boy from Cholavandan. None of them had anything to say. They too must have felt that the train was taking ages to come.

Dhanam's eldest uncle was the only person unaffected by the change of scene. Once he went behind a tree for a while. Then he took the kooja from Dhanam's mother, and drank a little water from it. When the temple bell pealed, he turned towards the temple and brought his palms together in worship. He went to the stationmaster's room and argued with him that the morsing was not the proper percussion accompaniment for nadaswaram music. But once he sighted the train, he became greatly excited.

The passenger train entered the railway station at a very slow pace, rather like the water flowing into the fields when the dam is opened. When it finally halted, one felt that it had no plans of leaving the place again. All the seven compartments were small four-wheeled ones. There were two compartments each of the first, second and third classes. One part of a third class coach was taken up by 'Spencers' Soda'. The doors of all the coaches opened only outwards.

In spite of there being a platform, they had to climb two steps to enter their compartment. Upon seeing a box and bedding being pushed into the third class compartment, the passengers who were already there put their legs up full length and lay down in their seats. Dhanam's uncle climbed in first, followed by Dhanam. Dhanam's mother got in last.

Dhanam's mother said to her younger brother on the platform, 'Go back home and take good care.' Her older brother patted awake one of the passengers lying on the bench and stacked their luggage on the bench. Though there were only ten people in the compartment, it was very stuffy. There were no signs of the train starting.

Dhanam sat by a window and looked out. There were four sets of benches facing each other that ran along the length of the compartment. Dhanam had to fold her legs and sit sideways to look out of the window.

Slowly at first, and then faster and faster, darkness began to fall. There were only two lights in the compartment and they were not lit.

Dhanam's uncle lost patience and opened the door to look out. Since the door opened outward, it was rather inconvenient to look out.

'Don't get down, annachi,' Dhanam's mother said. But he had already started to climb down. One of those people who were lying down sat up.

Neither the light inside the station room nor the single lamp post with an oil lamp shed much light. All the compartments of the train were quite dark.

Outside the station, a bullock-drawn, spring-axled carriage came to a stop with a jingle of bells. As if on cue, the lights of the train's compartments lit up.

Two people climbed down from the coach. They could see in the semi-darkness that one of them was wearing a coat and had a turban on his head. The stationmaster welcomed him shrinking obsequiously, and took the turbaned man to a first class compartment. A large box, a large bedding roll, a bamboo basket, and a mud pitcher fitted into a wooden frame with a handle—these things were carried into the train by the driver of the carriage and another man who had come with him. Together they took these things to the first class compartment that the turbaned gentleman had boarded. The stationmaster salaamed the turbaned man and walked away along the side of the train. Finding Dhanam's uncle standing out, he said, 'Hey, get inside the train.' After he reached the end of the train and spoke to someone, a whistle was heard. The train began to move at a leisurely pace.

Dhanam's uncle sat down beside her and began to chew betel leaves. Dhanam's mother was also looking out through the window. When at last no part of Vaitheeswarankoil was visible, she let out a sigh.

The train went forward very slowly, puffing out a lot of smoke and making a variety of metallic noises. Since night had fallen, and it was only three days past the new moon day, it was quite dark outside. The dim lights inside the train created a row of squares on the darkness on either side of the train. These lighted squares made visible the land and the cacti and other thorny bushes growing on it for just a moment and hastened on.

Dhanam watched the shadow of her head in the square of light shining through the window. It was moving with effortless ease over all the hillocks, plants and bushes. The train went its course, stopping at every station and starting unhurriedly. There were occasions when the station was not visible at all.

'Would you like to have your food now?' asked Dhanam's mother. Nobody seemed to get into their compartment at any station, though two people got down somewhere. The seven or eight left behind were enjoying a sound sleep.

Dhanam's mother brought up the subject of eating again. Without waiting for anyone's reply, she opened the bundle. Dhanam took the curd rice that her mother handed her on a piece of plantain leaf without a word. She must have somehow saved enough curd for the journey. That explained why the buttermilk they'd had for lunch had been more dilute than usual.

As Dhanam's uncle ate, her mother kept plying him with more and more curd rice from the pack. It did not seem to have been packed for just a single night's meal. She then cleared the bench for Dhanam to lie down. When Dhanam lay down with her legs well bent, she sat at her feet.

As Dhanam lay there with her ear pressed to the wooden plank of the bench, she could hear the noises made by the train clearly. Stout iron bars and chains hit and slid on each other. Then there was the rolling of the iron wheels on the rails, which sounded like some mega-percussion instrument.

The chill air and the noises produced by the train seemed to drag Dhanam into an endless cave. She had never seen a cave in all her life. A cave was something she had only heard about. A frequent visitor at their house always used the word in a sense that made one feel embarrassed.

At first Dhanam found the cave pitch dark. Nothing could be seen. But eyes that were used to seeing in the light got used to seeing in the darkness as well. The inside of the cave was rough on all sides. And the floor, uneven.

Suddenly it appeared that the cave was not that long after all. She was able to see quite well. At the end of the cave there was an upright stone. Even in this cave people seem to have consecrated a stone.

Dhanam moved closer to the stone. No need to move, really. It was there, just in front of her. Dhanam touched the stone.

The stone was soft. Dhanam passed her hand over the stone. It was not a stone, but a bundle of cloth. No, not a bundle of cloth either, it was a man. O God! I have touched some stranger!

But the man did not move. Was it a corpse? Her child, the one they had buried without letting her have even a glimpse —could it have been like this? Soft, smooth, but lifeless...

Repulsed, yet fascinated, Dhanam passed her hands again over the corpse. Head. Some hair. Big ears. Cheeks. Could even be a girl. But the hair was like that of a male. The eyes were closed. Large eyes. The eyeballs beneath the eyelids were motionless, peaceful. Nose—a large nose. There was slight warmth on one side of the nose. There was breath in that nostril. Lips. Chin. Why! Everything seems so familiar! Who is this? Who is this?

'Visu!' Dhanam woke up in a panic. Lost in the clanging of the passenger train, Dhanam's scream did not reach the ears of those who were sleeping.

It was past dawn when the train reached Chengalpet.

There was a small bathroom in a corner of the compartment. It had a tap at ankle-height, but no water. Following her uncle's hint to Dhanam's mother and at her mother's suggestion,

Dhanam visited the room once. But as soon as she entered the place, her whole body shrank. After that dream of last night, to keep her body breathing was all that she could do.

Dhanam kept watching through the window. The land was different here. The wind and the smells were not what she was familiar with. She could taste a salty tang in the air.

When the train stopped somewhere else, Dhanam's uncle got down unhurriedly, disappeared, and reappeared to get into the train. Another train sped past on the track beside their train. A few minutes after the other train had passed, their train began to move.

Opening a small trunk, Dhanam's mother took out a comb and a mirror, combed her hair and put a spot of pottu on her forehead. Seeing that Dhanam was watching listlessly through the window, she combed Dhanam's hair herself and wiped her face. The cloth she used for wiping turned black with the coal dust. Everyone's clothes were covered with coal particles. Though the train moved at the pace of a bullock cart, the quantity of smoke that it produced was enormous.

At last the train reached Egmore. Dhanam's mother got down first, holding the kooja and the basket. Her brother brought the trunks one by one to the door. The bedding roll had increased in size because it had not been properly tied. 'Dhanam, you get down,' he said. Dhanam climbed down slowly. The other passengers in the compartment got down after her.

Before Dhanam's uncle alighted, a man approached her mother and asked her, 'Do you want a coolie?'

Before she could answer, her brother intervened, 'No, we don't.'

But they did need his help. He wanted four-and-a-half annas to bring their luggage out of the station and hire a carriage for them. Beginning his bargain from one anna, Dhanam's uncle finally agreed to give two-and-a-half annas. With both the trunks placed on his head and carrying the bed and the basket in his hands, the coolie walked ahead. Dhanam, her mother and uncle followed him.

The place filled Dhanam with wonder. Huge iron beams had been crisscrossed and joined to provide spacious roofing for the station. The walls were like those of a fort. Wherever you looked, your eyes found the colour red. And wherever you looked, you found people. Many people wore turbans or hats. And these people—were these White people? What a variety of clothes! How do you distinguish between men and women among them? They looked as if they had no cares in this world.

The coolie made them cross the railway line to bring them out of the station. There were dozens of horse-drawn tongas standing outside the station. The drivers mobbed every passenger who came out. They would snatch away some piece of luggage from a passenger's hand and keep it in their carts. Two items of a single person's luggage were often loaded on two different tongas. The coolie who was carrying luggage went to one tonga, while Dhanam's mother was taken by a tonga-driver to his vehicle. With so many tongas closely parked in front of the station, it was difficult to know who went where. The people, the buildings, the horses, the stench of the place—everything was frightening. For a brief moment, when she was not able to see either her uncle or her mother, Dhanam experienced panic of the sort she had felt only as a child. Her sadness and longing, her desolation devoid of any expectations—were all replaced by a panic that filled her whole being.

Some seven or eight tonga-drivers were pulling the coolie who had brought their luggage in several different directions. But they were not able to break his firm resolve. All their luggage was loaded into a tonga chosen by him. 'Where do you want to go, sir?' asked the tonga-driver.

Nobody could figure out the address given by Dhanam's uncle. He said, 'I've been there. You just cross the railway gate, go straight, turn left, and there'll be a tank—that's the place.'

'Do you mean Purasavakkam, sir?'

'That's it! That's it.'

'Where in Purasavakkam, sir? Is it near the tank?'

They were not really convinced that the driver had understood the landmarks that Dhanam's uncle had been able to mention. 'Get in, we can search and locate the place,' the driver said.

The man who had brought their luggage from the station said, 'Will you let me go now, sir?'

Dhanam's uncle took out a snuff container from his waist and picked out a two anna coin and an one anna coin and gave them to him. The coolie gave back two quarter-anna coins.

Though the sun was quite hot, there were huge trees which provided shade unpierced even by a spot of sun. 'Dhanam, you get in first,' said her uncle.

At once the driver asked, 'Are you going to some place near Dhanathamma's house?'

'Yes, Yes. The street next to hers.'

'Why didn't you tell me that before, sir? That would be the second street on the left past the cinema hall. Get in, get in. Nothing to worry about now. We'll be there in a minute.'

Their faces brightened immediately. When Dhanam made to get into the tonga, the driver said, 'Let that lady get in. The young lady can get in after her.'

Dhanam's mother got in and sat down. Her uncle waited for the driver's word. 'Now ask the young lady to get in,' he said. 'Now sir, you get in and sit with your legs hanging out.' When he climbed in, it looked as if the carriage would tilt backwards. Immediately, the driver went to the front and took his seat. The vehicle regained its balance.

Though Dhanam did not get a seat convenient for looking out, she kept watching the scene eagerly, like a child. The streets were wider than necessary. At some places the houses were huddled close together. At other places, there were no houses at all. For the first time ever, she got a chance to see rickshas pulled by men. An occasional car was seen. And bicycles. There were trees on the road large enough to cover the entire width of the road with their shade. The driver kept talking to his horse, his chatter filled with both rebukes and endearments. Upon nearing the railway crossing, he took the horse across very carefully. The horse too obeyed his word like a child.

Dhanam's mother said to Dhanam, 'When you were just a child, I brought you along to visit all these places. How big the city has become now! What a lot of vehicles! There was a Mylapore lawyer who had sent a car for us. How grandly he celebrated that wedding! The pandal seemed to cover the whole city! No one in the vicinity had to light the stoves in their houses. Your uncle played the nadaswaram. And how! There was a confluence of great musicians for the wedding. Besides your uncle, another nadaswaram group and a band had also been hired. But the other nadaswaram player came and prostrated himself before your uncle and said, "In your presence I am not worthy even to play the pipe which would only produce a single note of the basic pitch." And he did not play at all. Mind you, he was older than your uncle. We went round the city in the car, visiting the beach, China Bazaar and other places—even though there was a war going on at that time.'

Dhanam's mind mused on what her mother had said. Her mother was speaking in this vein after such a long time, and Dhanam herself was listening with rapt attention. Boarding a train and coming to a strange city do effect a change in one's mind.

Their tonga reached another big road and turned. Dhanam looked at the driver's face. Looking at a male face like that was another thing she had not done for a very long time. His was an unfamiliar face, of course, but it also struck her as being somehow different. A small crowd had gathered by the roadside. Beneath the shade of a tree, a man in a long robe was making a speech. He spoke in Tamil, but with a difference. When their carriage had to go past him, the driver seemed to pull in the reins of the horse slightly. Within those few moments, the speaker had uttered the words, 'O you sinners!' two or three times. The driver appeared to pay attention to the speech even as he drove forward. Dhanam thought she understood—the driver belonged to some other religion—he was a christian.

She recollected something she had heard about that religion on some occasion. The railway journey had not only encouraged her to observe the outside world. It also brought back memories that she had relegated to oblivion, as being irrelevant to her—the christians do not cremate their dead. They dig graves in the earth and bury them, they do not let them be annihilated. They leave the body undisturbed. They go to heaven in their bodies, where they meet all those who left this world before them. There is room enough in that other world for all our dead. Unlike others, christians don't transmigrate as humans, nor are they reborn as tree or plant, insect or worm.

Craning her neck as much as she could, Dhanam kept looking at the preacher. The man will probably keep repeating 'O you sinners!' But, even if they are sinners, all those who are dead can meet each other again and talk, and shed tears of joy at some place, on some day. Instead of becoming ghosts and evil spirits that haunt tamarind and drumstick trees, it will be possible for us to meet our loved ones in our present forms.

Leaving the road, the carriage turned into a small lane. Dhanam felt a palpitating excitement—was all that really possible? Can we go to another world just as we are? Can we meet all those who died before us in that place? It must be a big world indeed. What a lot of people die everyday! Even on this train journey, had she not seen a number of corpses burning in various cremation grounds? She had no inkling who they were. Perhaps a man, or a woman or a child. Her child had not even been granted a proper end of this kind. It must have been bundled up in old clothes and thrown away somewhere. The child, too, must be waiting in that other world.

'This is the street. It is somewhere here,' said Dhanam's uncle.

The driver said, 'I told you I knew the place, sir. Didn't I?'

Dhanam looked the place over. Some of those houses looked like the houses in the villages with a wooden pillar and a niche on the wall for a lamp, near the threshold. Some of the houses were not like that. They looked as if the whole house had moved forward into the street. The kolam patterns drawn on the ground in front of the houses were mostly undisturbed as yet. Dhanam knew that the birds would be just waiting to peck away at the rice powder used for drawing the patterns in Vaitheeswarankoil. The design would be visible for some time after dawn. But most of it would vanish soon. Only those kolams drawn on festive occasions using rice paste and further decorated with bands of red clay would last longer.

During music practice at home, when her grandmother was alive, she often used to shout, 'Don't stray from the sruti.' Irrespective of whether the singers were young or old, the old woman would rebuke them in terms that would make one blush. If someone happened to be within reach, she would strike them too.

Once when her grandmother was in a genial mood, Dhanam had sat on her lap and asked her, 'Paati, what will happen if one strays from the sruti?' Dhanam was too young at that time to grasp what was meant by the basic pitch called sruti. Paati had stroked Dhanam's head. She had remained silent for a long while. Dhanam had asked her again. Adopting a demeanour suitable for the revelation of a great mystery, Paati whispered in her ear, 'If you sing without adhering to the basic pitch, you will be reborn as a donkey.' All that Dhanam was able to understand was that this was a matter of great importance, an impression she received from the manner in which her grandmother imparted it. At that age, she had no opportunity to find out anything about donkeys. Much later, the family went to Sirkazhi, where she'd observed a donkey carefully for the first time. It was still later that she had chanced to hear a donkey bray. By then she knew what sruti meant. And she was able to appreciate the importance of what her grandmother had said. Even while talking, if one's voice grew faint or if one gasped for breath, it sounds so unpleasant to the ears. So, for a singer, it must be a calamity indeed if the voice strays from the sruti. One could not say that everyone in her family sang well. Even Dhanam's mother was a mediocre singer. But none of them would stray the tiniest inflection from the basic pitch. The reason—Paati. And also the fear that oné would be born a donkey in the next birth. But that applies only if there really was rebirth. What if it was possible for us to go to the next world just as we are, retaining this same form?

'Welcome akka. Didn't Singaram meet you at the station?' enquired their relative, standing on the front steps of that house. And the tonga stopped.

Dhanam's uncle jumped down from the carriage. 'How are you Bhagyam?' he inquired. 'So you'd sent Singaram to the station, had you? We didn't see him at all. Poor fellow, must be searching for us somewhere.'

The driver got down and held the carriage steady. After Dhanam and her mother got down, he took their luggage down and carried it into the house.

'Here you are in Madras at last,' said Bhagyam. 'But why did you let your daughter get so anemic? First, have your bath and lunch and rest for a while. We can go out in the afternoon. There is a doctor nearby—Narayanaswamy Iyer. He has had an English education, but he prescribes medicines familiar to us, and also advises us on the diet we should follow. Let's take Dhanam to him. Anna, you look thinner than when you came here last month.'

Dhanam's uncle counted the items of their luggage and gave the driver his fare.

'How much did you give him?' asked Bhagyam.

'Six annas. Is that all right?'

'Quite. This fellow never demands exorbitant fares. You need the help of these tonga-drivers in this city.'

Dhanam moved towards the wall, feeling tired. The wall of the adjacent house rose tall across the central courtyard, cutting the house into two. The small courtyard had been roofed with a strong iron grill. It was an old-fashioned house, whitewashed recently. The veranda, though narrow, boasted of a swing. A wet cloth was drying on one side of the swing.

Bhagyam said, 'Go and brush your teeth, all of you. I'll make coffee for you. The rest can wait.'

Dhanam went and sat on the swing.

•———•

The misgivings that Dhanam's mother had secretly nurtured, did not come true. Dhanam's behaviour in Madras proved to be different from what everyone had grown accustomed to in Vaitheeswarankoil. She did not sit staring at the sky for hours together. Nor did she refuse to get up in the morning and end up spending the whole day in bed, as she had done several times in the past. Nor did she sit with tears streaming down her cheeks, breaking out into a racking sob now and again. Even when that dark boy, Visu had made his sudden appearances, which led to such embarrassment in their house, Dhanam's mother had borne it all without a frown on her face. Even though she had been deeply distressed when Dhanam had gone to Vaala's parents house and met such harsh treatment (the driver of the carriage had reported it on their return), she had not admonished Dhanam or blamed her. Upon hearing the news of Vaala's death, she too felt deeply grieved. She had even considered taking those children away, brahmin children though they were. At the same time, she also regretted that she could not rely on her daughter Dhanam. It was when Dhanam fell ill for the first time that a remark someone had made came to her mind again and again, 'Among women, some belong to the "caste of the chaste" whatever caste they are actually born into.' She often pondered over the truth of this remark.

A couple of days after they came to Madras, a man called Sitaraman came to their house. He had four notebooks with him. They were scripts. He made Dhanam sing for him, and then asked her to read out the part of a character from a play. Two days later, he gave her an advance of eighty rupees. Dhanam did not have to sing before huge audiences to exhibit her talent. This was a play, of course, but she did not have to wear makeup and costumes or share the stage with male actors and put up with their vulgar remarks and songs and jokes, on stage or off. All she had to do was to go to a silent recording room along with half-a-dozen people, sit there in front of a contraption that reminds her of a kitchen utensil (the long-handled iron ladle with holes for making boondi) and sing and speak from the script she held in her hand.

Sitaraman told Dhanam, 'One thing to be noted here is that each time you record, it has to be over in three minutes. The whole play will be divided into three minute segments for recording. The rehearsal will be quite strenuous. But then you have an advantage. You have the script in hand, which means that you don't have to worry about memorising. You don't have to put on greasepaint and appear before an audience. You can perform seated comfortably. But take care to maintain your face at the same distance from that boondi ladle. No shaking or turning of the face. You should not beat the tune audibly while singing. This expertise is not unattainable—you can do it quite easily. There is no big money in acting in these plays. But the time will come when you can cut separate records. And then there will be money—heaps of it.'

Within a month of coming to Madras, Dhanam had her first recording session. It was a play called *Manoranjitam* recorded on five gramophone records, that is, on ten sides. This play had everything in fours. Four princes. Four princesses. One prince was the hero and one princess, the heroine. All four princesses fall in love with the hero, one by one. He promises to meet them at four different hours of the night. The four princesses are accosted on their way by four different villains—an ogre, a highway robber, a shepherd.... And so the story proceeds. In the end everything works out happily. Someone joked that it would be apt if the play were to be produced in just four records. Everyone burst out laughing. The names of the four princesses were—Sarasi, Sallabi, Ullasi and Manoranjitam. Dhanam was given Ullasi's part. In addition, she also played a maid, a queen and a small boy. Musical accompaniment was to be provided by a harmonium and a tabla. All the princesses spoke and sang in a very high pitch.

Two months later came another play, *Paduka Pattabhishekam,* from the *Ramayana*. A famous actress was playing the part of Kaikeyi. A loud and ostentatious woman, she would come chewing betel leaves. She would chat with everyone, not differentiating between the old and the young.

Even those given to orthodox conventionalities were transformed in her presence. It was rumoured that she was very close to the proprietor of the gramophone company. Somebody even said that the two had got married.

Within six months Dhanam had taken part in three recorded plays known as 'drama sets'. Once, her mother noted that she hummed a tune from a play while she was tying her sari. Dhanam's uncle visited Vaitheeswarankoil and brought back some rice. He would go to the beach on foot and have his Tuesday's bath there. He joined a group of supervisors who were constructing a mansion for a zamindar on Poonamalli Road. When the old aunt left behind in Vaitheeswarankoil died, all three of them went there and stayed for sixteen days. Dhanam's mother later felt that they should not have gone there. The inside of the house wore an entirely different look. There were stains on the walls and cobwebs on the ceiling. Clothes hung from ropes tied haphazardly between the pillars on the inner veranda. There were two strangers who smoked cheroot even inside the house.

When Dhanam's mother tried to open the room she had left locked, the lock did not open at once. Only after the funeral rites were over and they had returned to Madras, did Bhagyam give the correct reason—someone must have tried to open the lock with another key. The lock had not yielded, though. It was solid and sturdy, but it must have been damaged inside. The house they had left behind in Vaitheeswarankoil was not like theirs any more. But it was apparent that Dhanam did not feel that way. Before the first day turned to night, the changes wrought on her by her stay in Madras vanished.

Once during those sixteen days Dhanam had asked her mother to arrange a bullock carriage for her. But it had not been possible. She then asked a boy with whom she was acquainted to look for Visu. The boy took two days to return.

Someone seemed to have told him that Vaala's parents household had moved to Thanjavur or Kumbakonam. The boy had not bothered to go to Kizhavur. He seemed to have met some relative of his with whom he spent a couple of days before returning to Vaitheeswarankoil.

When the carriage arrived in front of their house to take them to the railway station, Dhanam and her mother had but one thought. Last time, it was at this juncture that the dark boy had materialised from somewhere. Will he come this time?

The bullock carriage crawled along. The road was quite muddy after the rains. The station was not very far from their house. Visu had come from the opposite direction last time. From inside the carriage Dhanam and her mother were both looking in the same direction now. But Visu did not come. Even after the train came and they boarded it, Dhanam kept looking towards the town. The train started. Dhanam's eyes continued to search for Visu. Visu did not come.

Inside the train, Dhanam began to sob. Even her mother felt that though Dhanam was no better than a walking corpse in her sorrow, she had been inexplicably infused with some mysterious power till now. It seemed to have left her, all of a sudden.

This time, Egmore railway station offered no cause for wonder. The air did not feel new. As for the people, they seemed to have become invisible.

Scarcely a week after this second arrival at Madras, Dhanam began to cough a little. Practically everyone they met seemed to have fever and cold at that time. Dhanam did not seem to have caught a cold, but she had a cough. With two doses of a herbal decoction it disappeared.

The play *Kovalan*, based on the epic *Silappadikarum*—which deals with the love of a chaste wife as well as a courtesan, for Kovalan—was to be produced as a 'drama set' of twelve records. Though the hero's wife happens to be Kannagi, it was the courtesan Madhavi who had the lead female role in the play. Madhavi's part was found in seven records, not absent even on a single side. Kannagi, the wife, spoke her first words only on side thirteen, where she pointed to various pieces of jewellery and asked her maid, 'What's this? And what's this?' When she finally came to inquire about the mangalyam, which is tied by the groom round the bride's neck during the wedding, she had been given her first song. Later there was a duet when Kovalan returns home after leaving Madhavi and has to sell Kannagi's anklet. The song went, 'Is there no one who would buy this in all the towns of Mayavaram, Kumbakonam or Thanjavur?'

Dhanam was rehearsing for Kannagi's part. Madhavi's part was to be played by that notorious actress who was close to the proprietor of the gramophone company. But for some reason the actress herself chose to exchange parts. That she was at the final stage of pregnancy could have been one of the reasons.

There was a song assigned to Madhavi on the second side of the second record, where she sings to Kovalan, 'Get up and come with me, my lord.' During the final rehearsal of this song, Dhanam was seized by a sudden fit of coughing. A drop of saliva from her mouth sprayed on the freshly laundered veshti of the man who was playing Kovalan. He did not bother about it. But someone who had noticed it pointed it out in a rather peculiar manner. The spot had become a saffron-coloured dot. And everyone knew that Dhanam was not in the habit of chewing betel leaves.

Bhagyam was the one who was most distressed by this. She reproached herself, 'The day you arrived I said I'd take her to the doctor. Curse me! I haven't done it till today. And look at the plight it has led her to!' Those were the days when doctors themselves wrote off tuberculosis patients. The disease was in an advanced stage in Dhanam's case. Lurking in her body for two or three years, it must have eaten away her lungs.

Cow's milk and Indian medicines like chyavanaprash and bhasma did not effect any great change in her. A reputed doctor—one who was suited and booted—advised them to shift to some place near Tambaram. He said that the disease was infectious; Dhanam must always be made to spit in a receptacle which should be kept covered. The sputum should be buried deep everyday, he added.

They finally decided not to go to Tambaram but to go back to their own place. Dhanam's mother brought Dhanam to Vaitheeswarankoil, travelling first class. There was quite a big crowd residing in their house now. A small room was vacated and Dhanam was laid on a cot. There were times when the presence of so many people at home acted as an irritant; but there were also times when everyone was needed. However, on one occasion Dhanam's mother blurted out, 'What a lot of eyes to express disgust when a woman in her prime lies bedridden!'

However, there was little cause for anyone to feel unduly afraid or disgusted, for it so happened that early one night, four days after reaching Vaitheeswarankoil, Dhanam died, not having uttered a single word or expressed a single wish. Some woman remarked that it was at the same hour past sunset that Yama, the god of death, had appeared, when he came for Venkatachalam and his wife Vaala. After keeping a night-long vigil, the first thing that Dhanam's mother did in the morning was to send word to Kizhavur.